Celina MacNeill, da [...]
Tor, to be sold to the [...]

For Celina it all se [...]
auction is as real as [...]
Culloden, the defeat of her prince, Charles Stuart, and
her transportation to the West Indies.

Her final humiliation is to be owned by Captain Nicholas
Benedict, whose reputation as a privateer leaves her in
little doubt that she is to be subjected to his basest
whims. But the Captain has another fate in store for
her—and Celina soon finds that willing servitude can be
even better than freedom!

ELUSIVE
FLAME OF LOVE
VALENTINA LUELLEN

MILLS & BOON LIMITED
London · Sydney · Toronto

First published in Great Britain 1984
by Mills & Boon Limited, 15–16 Brook's Mews,
London W1A 1DR

ISBN 0 263 74827 8

Set in 10 on 12 pt Linotron Times
04–0984–62,750

Photoset by Rowland Phototypesetting Ltd
Bury St Edmunds, Suffolk
Made and printed in Great Britain by
Cox & Wyman Ltd, Reading

CHAPTER ONE

CELINA SAW him as she was being roughly herded towards the auction platform which had been erected at the end of the quay. He stood at the back of the gaping crowd of onlookers already gathering for the first sale of the day. She recognised him immediately as the man who had watched the prison ship from Tilbury being unloaded the previous day. She had passed within a few feet of him then, shackled, dirty, unkempt after weeks at sea during which she wished herself dead a thousand times, and, unlike many others who moved back contemptuously—a few perhaps pitying the bedraggled spectacles of humanity being paraded before them, he had stood quite still, apparently untouched by the squalidness of their condition.

In the fierce sunlight which had almost blinded her after she had been dragged from the punishment cell and brought up on deck for the first time in over two weeks, she remembered his eyes, of the most startlingly brilliant blue she had ever seen. They had been the first thing she noticed about him. Cold, expressionless eyes set in a sun-bronzed face that could not be called handsome; perhaps, rather, strong. A face of character and determination. His gaze had centred first on the tangled mass of hair, as black as a raven's wing, which shadowed her thin face, before wandering down over her body in a

slow almost insulting stare that brought instant colour to
her ashen cheeks. For the first time in over a year she felt
like a woman again! What neither the rough sailors with
their crude remarks and furtive caresses out of sight of
the captain had failed to achieve, nor the more subtle
advances of the officers, who were often worse than the
ranks because of the authority they had, this man had
accomplished with a single look.

She could feel those piercing eyes on her now, as she
stood in line with the other poor wretches waiting to be
sold. As if compelled by some unseen force she raised
her head and found his gaze full on her, disturbing in its
intensity. She was clean at last. She had been allowed to
bathe and wash her hair, but no one had thought to
provide a comb or mirror, and her skin had been rubbed
dry by a coarse towel. She had thought of refusing, but
her gaolers had threatened to strip and wash her themselves, and the fear of this had been sufficient to make
her comply. Her back still bore the bruises from the
attack on her ten days before. She wanted no more. She
had been given a clean dress too. Clean! It smelt vile.
She looked down at the drab grey calico a size too small
and was immediately overcome with shame. The tight
bodice cut low across her breasts revealed more of them
than any ball-gown she had ever owned. The skirt,
curving over shapely hips that were exceedingly slender
after months of inadequate food, ended at least three
inches above her bare feet. She had been thrown a pair
of shoes, but they pinched her toes after being so long
barefoot, and the girl next to her had swooped on them
as if they had been a tasty morsel of food. When they
tried to force her feet into another pair, she had swung
her manacled hands at the head of the nearest guard and
cut his face. Even shackled, she had learned to give a

good account of herself.

For that misdemeanour she had been knocked unconscious and thrown into a windowless room together with half a dozen other troublemakers and deprived of food and water that night and this morning. She felt faint with hunger and fear.

She was to be sold as an indentured servant! Celina MacNeill, daughter of Malcolm, Laird of Craig Tor and his gentle wife Margaret. The last surviving member of her family to suffer at the hands of the English. Sold to the highest bidder! To work as a kitchen-maid, a seamstress or scullion. She had been the only lady of rank among the prisoners transported this trip. Not that she had been afforded any privileges because of it. She had been pushed into an overcrowded cell with the other women, forced to live like an animal, think like an animal, until it was hard to remember what life had been before that day in the heather when she and David had been captured by Cumberland's troopers.

Beside her were labourers, shoemakers, carpenters. Several gentlemen who had fared no better than she had, for all her genteel upbringing, now stood in chains alongside her. Most of the women prisoners had committed no worse a crime than to follow their men into battle. Camerons, MacDonalds, Stewarts, Frasers. Such proud Highland names. Such stalwart young men who had gone off to war, now reduced to pathetic shadows destined for a life of servitude.

The voyage from England had been a nightmare, but this was worse, Celina thought. The way the women stared at her, whispered behind gloved hands and fluttering fans. She could guess what they were saying and hated them for their narrow-mindedness. She knew that in the ill-fitting dress she looked like a woman of the

streets. But it had not been so long ago when she had
worn the finest French silks and Brussels lace, and
diamonds had sparkled at her throat and in her ears.
Like the night she had met Charles Stuart in Edinburgh.
She closed her mind against the painful memories which
came flooding back. The Prince, that handsome, gentle
young man who had won the hearts of men, women and
children alike wherever he went, and had brought
thousands flocking to his banner. Her brother, dead
now, along with her father and mother and Maura, her
sister. The massacre of Culloden, their home in flames,
the months of hiding in the hills until, near-dead from
starvation, they had been captured by soldiers and tried
along with so many others for treason against the
English King.

Tried and found guilty. Sentenced to seven years as an
indentured servant and transportation! It was the one
word which brought dread to every Scottish heart after
the failure of the 1745 uprising. Somehow she had
survived it, but it had changed her. Now she was like an
empty shell in which nothing lived. No hope, no emo-
tions, nothing. It had all been taken from her. Family,
home, security, love!

For weeks she had not known where she was to go,
and then the captain of the prison ship broke it to them
all. Antigua. From there, depending on who bought
them, the prisoners could be scattered throughout the
West Indies, even shipped to the American colonies.

The crowd moved closer as a uniformed officer and
several soldiers arrived. Sheets and sheets of parchment
were unrolled on to a large table. Names began to be
read out. MacDonald, shoemaker. He was sold for nine
pounds sterling. A young woman with a baby in her
arms, registered under the name of the regiment she had

followed—Isabel MacIan, whose man had fought with
the Clanranald MacDonalds. Her master was assured
she could both spin and knit and was of a mild disposition. Could she be anything else with a child to rear,
Celina thought sadly, watching her walk away. Her
price? Fifteen pounds. The prospect of a lusty boy to do
full-time work alongside his mother in a few years had
greatly increased the price.

Donald MacNeill, from South Uist, as she was herself.
Labourer. He had two fingers missing. Six pounds only.
Six pounds! Was that the price of a human life in this
God-forsaken place, she thought in horror.

The names went on and on. People shuffled past her
and were led away. The line dwindled. She was one of
the last, but the inevitable was growing closer and closer.

There was a lull in the proceedings. Men began climb-
ing up on the platform to inspect some of the remaining
prisoners. Celina's head was roughly jerked back from
behind. She gasped in pain. Fingers probed her mouth,
prising it open. The reek of brandy fumes full in her face
made her want to be sick.

'This one,' a voice said in her ear, and her stricken
gaze focused on a middle-aged man, balding, well
dressed, but coarse for all his finery, she thought, by the
way he had manhandled her. 'Does she have a name?'

'Celina MacNeill.' The officer looked up after scouring
his parchment for several minutes. 'She's listed here as
being of good stock.'

'Shame on you, Lester, and you a married man.' The
tall stranger vaulted on to the platform with the agility of
a mountain cat. Close to, Celina realised he was over six
feet tall and very well built beneath his elegantly styled
clothes. A froth of white lace at his throat accentuated
the swarthiness of his skin. But he was no dandy, she

decided, forcing herself to look up into those blue eyes. He was a man who knew what he wanted from life and would not be afraid to reach out and take it. And he was looking at her! He nodded in the direction of the officer. 'Captain Grayson, how are you? Have you anything which might interest me?'

'I doubt that, Captain Benedict. I thought you had filled your quota last week?'

'Apart from a few house-servants. This one here, for instance,' he indicated Celina with a gesture of his hand. A large solitaire diamond ring flashed in the sunshine as he reached into a pocket, produced a silver case and extracted a long black cheroot. 'Would she do?'

'This one? She's a troublemaker, Captain, that's why the shackles are still on her. Tried to kill one of the officers who went below to give her food and water in the punishment cell. She spent most of her time there, I hear. A real hellion among the men, caused no end of trouble.' The English officer gave a sly smile. 'A taste of the whip might tame her, or the right man, but as for putting her among decent people trying to do a day's work . . . !'

"I think she is just what I need. I'll take her.' The balding man released Celina's hair and she swayed dazedly, suddenly very much afraid. He did not want her to work, but to warm his bed. At her sharp intake of breath, the man called Benedict stared at her closely. What did she see in those eyes? Was he waiting for her to beg him to buy her instead of the other drink-sodden man? She did not know how to beg. Even when she had been beaten, she had not cried out. What did it matter who owned her? They would own a body, not her soul. It would give her master no pleasure if he chose to use it for his own satisfaction.

'Just a moment, my friend. We are both interested in purchasing this merchandise,' the captain drawled softly.

Merchandise! They were discussing her as though she was a sack of potatoes, Celina thought, bristling with indignation. Had she no rights? No, she had nothing of her own any more. Rights, honour, liberty, all would belong to whoever purchased her.

'I'll make an offer of three pounds. If she's a trouble-maker, she's not worth more,' the balding man said.

'And in what capacity do you intend using her?' Captain Benedict asked, looking amused. 'I can just see her sitting at Martha's side, taking instruction in sewing. Would your wife appreciate such a companion?'

'I sew very well,' Celina said in a low tone, hating them both.

'Do you, now. And what other talents do you possess, my dear?' Thick fingers were laid on her arm until she jerked it away in disgust.

'I should think they are obvious to anyone who looks at her. No, Lester, you are too old for her. You'd never tame a wildcat like this. I'll give you six pounds, Captain Grayson.'

'Eight.' The bald man's face grew red, as someone in the crowd tittered with laughter.

'Ten. I mean to have her, so stop now before you get in over your head.' Captain Benedict sent a cloud of blue-grey smoke into the air with a shrug of broad shoulders.

'Like father, like son, eh? Young and pretty, that's how you both like your women, isn't it? I'm surprised you have to sink to this level to find one. Are pickings lean in the Caribbean these days?'

A well-aimed balled fist caught the balding man on

the jaw, knocking him to the ground, where he lay unconscious.

'I offered ten pounds, Captain Grayson. Is my bid accepted?' Through narrowed eyes Captain Benedict watched two soldiers carry the man to the back of the platform and begin to revive him. He showed not the least sign of anger or concern at what had taken place, Celina thought. What kind of man was he?

'Have it your own way, Captain. The girl is yours.'

'Strike her chains, then, and I'll take her with me. I sail on the tide.'

Already he was turning away. He had got what he wanted—her—and now it was as if she was of no interest to him. She struggled to retain her fading senses. The sun on her unprotected head had made her feel sick. The knowledge that she was now the property of this stranger instead perhaps of some genteel woman who might have taken her into her family, and understood her position, crushed a last pathetic hope that she might regain her freedom. An indentured servant for seven long years. She could not stand it!

'I'll send Xavier to you with the money within the hour.'

'I think I can trust you, Captain Benedict. Are you sure about her chains? After what I've told you?'

'I assure you I am man enough to handle her,' came the soft amused reply.

He stood by while Celina's chains were removed. They had left ugly red marks on her skin, and in many places it was raw. The man who had bought her lifted one slender wrist and frowned at what he saw.

'You'll not wear those again, but I give you fair warning, girl. Behave yourself or you'll answer to me. Do you understand?'

She nodded and his frown grew at her silence, sensing it as deliberate.

'Answer me! I know you are no mute.'

'I understand perfectly. I am your property. How little value you place on human life!'

'Because I paid only ten pounds for you?' He looked at her, surprised by the unexpected show of spirit. She had a quiet voice, with a gentle lilt to it that reminded him of the sea. What was her background, he wondered. Was she one of the women who had followed her man to war? Lost him perhaps in battle? Or, beneath the sullen attitude, was there more to this girl called Celina MacNeill? 'From what Grayson told me, it was too much.'

'Then why did you bother to waste your money?'

'Are you telling me you would rather have gone with Lester? He isn't a very subtle character, is he? You read his mind as I did. Is that what you wanted? To be in his bed?'

'No! No more than I wish to be in yours,' Celina cried, and his eyes gleamed.

'So there is spirit in you still. I'm glad. For a moment I thought I had a mouse on my hands. Resent me if you must. Hate me. It's of no consequence to me so long as you do as you are told.' Her arm was taken in a firm grasp and she was propelled through the crowd and away from the quay so fast that she had to run to keep up with his long strides.

She was aware of people staring at her. Saw pity in the eyes of some of the women, which greatly heightened the apprehension mounting inside her. They thought as she did! Where was he taking her? Dear heaven, she felt so weak she could scarcely breathe, and her steps lagged. A slave to the whims of this man who held her.

She had to escape. Perhaps she would find someone with a sympathetic ear who would hide her. Desperation bordering on panic gave her false hope, false courage, strength to legs that moments before had wanted to collapse beneath her. At the first opportunity, she told herself. What if there wasn't one? What if she was taken aboard his ship immediately, given no chance to flee.

'Wait here for me, I'll be a moment only.' Captain Benedict halted before a waterfront inn, motioned her to sit down on a low wall alongside it and went inside. For several minutes she stared after him, not realising her good fortune, then she took to her heels and ran.

She had only one thought in her mind—to get away from the quayside and anyone who might recognise her and return her to her master. The cobblestones burned the soles of her bare feet, to which fear had lent wings. A sharp pain made her cry out and, looking down, she saw she had cut her right foot on some broken glass. She limped on, her chest near to bursting at the exertion which weakened her already starved and abused body, into a narrow alley where the buildings were close together, shutting out the fierce sunlight. She had to stop and rest, or she would collapse. No, she must not. Ruthlessly she forced herself on. Voices, shouting behind her, made panic sweep through her like wildfire. Her escape had been discovered.

'Here, girl. Where do you think you're going?' A burly man stepped out of a doorway in front of her. She screamed as hands reached out to grasp her, oblivious to the fact it would bring Captain Benedict after her for sure. 'Come here, now. Runaway, by the looks of you.'

A hairy arm went around her waist, lifting her from the ground. Another covered her mouth. She sank her teeth into it with all the ferocity she could muster, and was released as the man gave a savage oath and flung her from him.

'Why, you little vixen I'll . . .'

'My property, I believe. I'll take her now.' Captain Benedict stood at the entrance to the alley, at his side a tall, half-naked negro. As he started towards her, Celina turned and ran again, heard him order, 'Come back, you little fool. There's nowhere you can go.'

He was right. It was a blind alley. Before her was a sheer wall. Closed doors on both sides and behind her! Sobbing, she reached for a stone at her feet, turned with her back against the wall, waiting. He would not take her! He would not!

'No, Xavier, leave her to me.' His companion was waved back. 'Must I come and fetch you, Celina?'

The new note in his voice was menacing, challenging her brave stand. The stone she held rose higher as he stepped closer, but it did not deter him.

'I'll use it. I won't go with you. I won't! You have no right to own me,' she cried. He was so close he could reach out and take it from her. Close enough for her to strike him. Her hand trembled. First him, then the others when they came to take her. And then she looked into his eyes and knew she was beaten. Whatever she did, he would still take her with him. She was his property and he would not be cheated out of his purchase. It was written there for her to see and understand—and accept, or pay the consequences.

'This time I will overlook your foolishness, but if it happens again, you will not find me a patient man.' Lean brown fingers snaked out to grasp her wrist. The pain of them tightening around her injured flesh made her senses reel. She pitched forward into his arms, felt herself lifted and thrown across his shoulder. 'Go and settle with Captain Grayson, Xavier, while I get this wench aboard. She'll give me no more trouble.'

Wench! A nobody, carried through the streets across his shoulder for everyone to see. Celina was spared the humiliation of the spectacle, for she was barely conscious during the short walk back to his ship. Only when she felt herself set down again did she open her eyes and make some effort to recover her composure.

'Give her some food. Something light at first. Broth will be enough.' Captain Benedict was lounging in a huge leather chair beside the open latticed window, talking to a young woman whose skin was the colour of dark honey. She wore a white cotton blouse pushed down over smooth shoulders, a long red checked skirt and leather sandals on her bare feet. Shining mahogany hair was swept high on her head and covered with a white handkerchief edged with lace. 'Did you manage to get her some clothes?'

'Enough to make her look more presentable for the time being.' The voice had an attractive husky quality about it. 'There will be more time to buy things for her in Kingston.'

'You know what I want. Get it for her.'

What he wanted! She would not wear anything he bought, Celina thought as she raised herself on one elbow. She was in a pleasantly furnished cabin, lying on a small bed along one wall. The sheets beneath her aching body were real silk. How long had it been since she had felt such luxury against her skin? A year? No, more like two. She had been a fugitive with David in the heather for six months after the battle of Culloden and then in prison for another four. If she counted the months at sea, at least two years! Time had slipped away without her realising it.

'So you have recovered?' Captain Benedict was staring across at her. Slowly she sat up, not answering, and saw a warning line crease his brows. Be careful, it told her. You have had your one and only chance. 'Are you hungry?'

'Yes, very.' Why should she lie? Food would give her strength, new life. Strength to fight against the bondage he had forced on her.

'Good. I'm glad to see you are going to be sensible and accept what has happened to you.'

'I did not say that. I shall never accept it,' Celina said in a fierce whisper.

'Then be prepared for a few stormy passages ahead, my little Scots cat. You'll not leave your mark on me like you did on the first officer of the prison ship. Do you want me to break you, Celina MacNeill? I shall succeed where others have failed, have no doubt of that.' His words chilled her and he saw her draw back as though she had been struck. With a gesture of annoyance he ground out the cheroot he was smoking and climbed to his feet. 'I'll be on deck if you have any trouble with her, Sulai.'

As the door slammed shut behind him, the woman came across to where Celina sat and smiled down at her.

'Don't mind him none, child, you've ruffled his feathers a little, that's all. He's a good man at heart.'

'I hate him.' Celina did not respond to the show of friendship. To do so would mean that she was prepared to accept what was happening to her.

'Now why should you? Hasn't he taken you out of those chains, given you a new life?' came the surprised reply.

'You don't understand. How could you?'

'What makes you think we are different?' Sulai stared at her with serious eyes. 'We are both his property, child. I don't hate him. He's the best master I've ever had. I won't ever do anything to make him sell me. Get off that bed, now, and come with me. I've a bath all prepared and some clean clothes. Something you will like better than that thing you have on. Well, don't just sit there. For heaven's sake, are you going to be difficult? He expects it. I've orders to get you cleaned up even if I have to get a couple of men in to help me. You don't want that, do you?'

Silently Celina shook her head and huge tears rolled down over her cheeks as the full extent of her position came home to her.

'I see you understand how foolish it would be to go against him!' Sulai gently helped her from the bed, tutting as she saw the marks on her wrists, the blood on her foot. 'You need some taking care of, child. Trust Sulai.'

What other choice had she, Celina thought miserably as she allowed herself to be led into an adjoining cabin where an enormous tub, half-full of steaming hot water, awaited her. The grey calico was stripped from her, with more vexed exclamations from Sulai at the sight of her thin body, the bruises still visible on her back and shoulders.

'Who put these marks on you, child?' In all the months which followed, she was never to call Celina anything else, although barely three or four years could have separated them in age. It was a term of affection, Celina came to realise, from someone older and wiser in the ways of the world. She learned to listen and appreciate the words of wisdom, of experience, that came her way. At the moment these were lost on her in her state of apathy. 'Men! Most of them have no idea how to treat a woman.'

'How does your Captain Benedict treat a woman?' Celina asked. The heat of the water was turning her skin a bright red, but she stood it, feeling it steal into her aching limbs and offering blessed relief. Without wanting to, she began to relax as Sulai soaped her all over, taking extra care with her hair.

'That depends entirely on the woman herself. If you are sensible you will make life easy for yourself. Be nice to him, and you'll not find him a hard master or an ungenerous one. With what you have to offer a man, you will be able to ask for anything you want.'

'Except my freedom.'

'What he is offering you isn't exactly slavery, child. Even if I were free, I wouldn't leave his house. I like it there and I'm well treated. I have everything I want.'

'When I am free, *then* I will have what I want,' Celina said, emerging to allow herself to be towelled dry. The soft texture of the cloth against her body was a far cry from the roughness which had last touched it. What was she being offered, she wondered, as Sulai slipped a crisp white shift over her head and then a taffeta petticoat before helping her into a dress of pale lilac silk.

'He was right. The colour goes with those eyes of yours. What a colour they are. You should wear violet and dark greens and yellow to show off that beautiful hair,' the woman said as she stepped back to examine the appearance of her charge. 'A definite improvement. There's a mirror in the other room. Go and look at yourself, and then tell me you don't like what you see.'

Limping slightly in new leather shoes of dark indigo with silver buckles, Celina obeyed her. The girl staring back at her from the glass was a stranger. Thin-faced, pale-cheeked, long black hair flowing past her shoulders, clean, but lacking the lustre it had once known.

'You will soon fill out with good food inside you,' Sulai assured her, 'and the sun will put colour into those cheeks. I have salve for your wrists at home and something to make your hair shine again. In a few weeks you will be your old self again.'

No, she would never be that again, Celina thought, as she sat down to eat the bowl of thick broth in front of her, floating with pieces of meat and vegetables, the sight of which made her stomach growl noisily. The slop served on board the prison ship had been fit only for pigs, and she had refused to touch it at first, but eventually she had been forced to eat in order to stay alive. How easy it would be to accept that she was now a servant, but at the back of her mind was still the nagging fear she had not been bought to become a mere servant at the beck and call of Captain Benedict. She had the impression that that had not been his true reason for parting with ten pounds.

'You didn't tell me who marked you?' Sitting opposite her, Sulai watched her eat, marvelling at her self-control. She sensed Celina could have fallen on the meal, simple though it was, like an animal, such was her hunger, but she did not. Each mouthful was carefully savoured and appreciated. She was no ordinary woman, she decided, but someone of breeding, if not of rank, back in Scotland. From what Sulai had heard of the place, she had always considered it to be a wild, barbaric country, yet something inside her had been stirred when news of Charles Stuart's failure to succeed in his attempt to seize the crown of both England and Scotland reached Jamaica. Many of Scots descent in the island had shed a

tear and drunk his health across the water. She had
known a doctor from Skye who had returned there to
offer his services to his Prince. A mild-mannered man,
yet with such devotion to the country of his birth that he
had been prepared to return and offer his life in its
service.

Celina MacNeill was made of such stuff. She had
suffered, but she would survive. A man of insight, a
gentle man, could bring her back to life again, make her
forget the past and all she had lost. From the expression
in those lovely eyes, a mixture of blue and violet,
touched sometimes with grey, she had lost a great deal.
It was as Sulai had said to Xavier, when the captain had
come to the inn and told them of his purchase and
instructed her to buy clothes for the girl. Why had he
bought her? We need no more help at the house. As
always, Xavier turned his mean look on her for daring to
question the wishes of the man he served and, as usual,
she ignored the warning. She was not afraid of him, for
all his importance. 'The captain always has a reason for
everything he does,' he had replied blandly, and Sulai
had laughed at that. 'One day that man will do something without good reason—for himself maybe,' she
mused, and the frown on Xavier's ebony face had
grown. 'If he wishes to take a woman for himself, that is
his right. But what would he want with this thing, skin
and bones, when he has a fine lady in Kingston to warm
his bed?'

What indeed, Sulai wondered as she cleared the table.
Perhaps that day had come when Nicholas Benedict had
done something without a practical reason. This girl was
pretty. When she filled out she would be attractive. In a
month or two, with Sulai's carefully tuition, she would
be as beautiful as she suspected she had once been. She

would wear fine silks and lace, and jewels would en-
hance that soft, pale skin. The captain would not regret
his purchase if Sulai had her way.

'Why are you looking at me like that?' Celina asked
suddenly, and Sulai gave a soft laugh. She had still
offered no explanation for the marks on her, and she did
not intend to.

'Thoughts, child. My own thoughts. Would you like
some air? Go up on deck for a while. This isn't a prison
ship, you know.'

'It is to me, but I think I will. Will—will he be up
there?'

'At the helm, child. The captain has his father's blood
in him,' and Sulai laughed again as she ushered her out
of the cabin.

What had she meant by that, Celina wondered, as she
climbed the stairs. Then a refreshing breeze from the sea
hit her and she heard the waves crashing against the bow
of the ship as she clove her way through the water.
Suddenly all else was forgotten. Blindly she groped her
way to the rail, clung tightly to it as she closed her eyes,
and allowed memory to engulf her. The house on the
cliffs where she had been born. Her first memory was of
the sound of the sea, the wind howling about the headland where Craig Tor had stood. Where broken stones
and graves were all that remained of a once proud house,
birthplace of her brother, her father and his father
before him. Stronghold of the MacNeills of Craig Tor.
All gone now, to waste and destruction, back to the
earth from which it had risen. It would never rise again,
for there was no one to rebuild.

The wind stung her eyes and she felt tears on her
cheeks. Tears for the land she would never see again.
The heritage she had lost! Below her, the sea pounded

against the side of the ship as it had done against the cliffs below the house. How easy it would be to lean over a little more and then a little more, to allow herself to fall and be swallowed up in the frothy waves. No servant, then, but free. She was meant to be free!

'Do you value your life so little?' Captain Benedict was at her side, his eyes betraying the fact that he had read her thoughts, but he made no attempt to touch her. She realised she had reached up on tip-toes ready to plunge herself into the green depths and end her life for ever. 'Throw yourself over, then. I'll not stop you.'

'You—you would not?' His words stunned her. 'And lose your investment, Captain?' Scorn came quickly on the heels of her surprise. 'How lucky you are to be able to toss away ten pounds. If I had had that much, I might have saved my brother's life while he was rotting in prison, but all our money had gone and I could not buy him food when he fell ill, could not pay to stop them from dragging him away. Oh, God! How lucky you are.'

He pressed something into her hands. Startled, she found herself looking at the grey calico dress in which she had been sold.

'Throw that overboard instead, Celina, together with the past. Begin a new life,' he said quietly. As if pushed by an unseen hand, she allowed the garment to fall from her grasp over the side. It floated out behind the ship and then disappeared into the white-topped waves and was lost to view. She hated him for the hold he had over her. Her only retaliation was to attack the gesture.

'There, Captain. Your wish is my command.'

'I thought you had learned your lesson. You will get nowhere using that tone with me. Get below again and stay there until you find your manners,' came the harsh command, and she picked up her skirts and moved away from him, her pale face expressionless. 'And stay away from my crew. I've warned them of your reputation, so you'll get no help from that quarter.'

Warned them against her! She was swept with shame. Was she to be for ever labelled as a wanton? She turned and looked at the man behind her. He stood with the sun behind him, which turned his thatch of blond hair almost to white. A withering look which had, in the past, reduced men to shameful silence!

'I am not accustomed to seeking the company of common seamen, Captain, whatever you have heard.' Her voice shook with anger. Captain Benedict's eyes gleamed as he heard it. Each time he baited her, she showed a little more spirit. It had been suppressed too long in her and needed to be released.

'Then you shall have my company tonight, Mistress MacNeill,' he mocked, hands on hips. 'My cabin, eight o'clock. We shall dine together.'

'I will not,' Celina breathed. Men were watching the encounter, smiling at each other as they assessed the outcome. None of them gave anything for her chances, she thought bitterly.

'Sail on the port bow!' Above them the lookout's voice rang loud and clear, diverting all attention from her plight.

Captain Benedict turned on his heel, shading his eyes against the glare of the sun to inspect the ship bearing down on them at a fast rate.

'It's the *Diamant*.' Xavier was at his side, handing him his spyglass.

'So she's still lurking in these waters. Hoping for another prison ship, no doubt. I cannot afford a fight, much as I'd like one.' He turned and saw Celina staring wide-eyed at the second ship, and smiled into her anxious features. 'Don't worry, they'll not take you from me.'

'Who are they?'

'A French man o'war. They intercepted another prison ship not long ago within landfall of Antigua and took the prisoners to Martinique and freed them.'

'Captain, look!' Xavier exclaimed, catching his arm. A larger, more heavily built ship, which dipped low in the water, was cutting its way between their own vessel and the Frenchman.

'By God, it can't be! It is! The "Fox" is back in home waters, Xavier! We can go on our way now without fear of being intercepted.' Captain Benedict chuckled, and his obvious pleasure at the sight of the strange ship drew Celina to the rail to watch the engagement. The French man o'war had veered away with the other in close pursuit. She heard the bark of a cannon and saw smoke drift into the cloudless blue sky.

'We shall be able to dine in peace this evening, Mistress.'

She ignored the hateful smile on his face as he glanced at her, and asked hesitantly, 'You know that ship, too?' What manner of man was he? What did he do? He seemed to know a great deal about the sea and the men who sailed it.

'And its captain. He is my best friend. The "Fox" is what you might call a privateer, and a very successful one,' came the amused reply.

'A pirate!' she gasped, stepping back from him. 'Is that what you are?'

'What if I were? A pirate could give you fine clothes and jewels, perhaps a great house which would match these airs and graces. If you were a lady and not a common little tramp, as I know you are, then you would have thanked me long before this for not leaving you to the tender mercies of that drunken lecher, Lester. Or are you waiting for a suitable time? Tonight perhaps? Eight o'clock, remember, and I dislike unpunctuality.'

And with that parting shot, he left her, and went up on the bridge.

CHAPTER
TWO

NICHOLAS TURNED to look at the girl Xavier admitted to his cabin punctually on the stroke of eight, and a smile touched his lean mouth as he saw the smouldering resentment in her eyes quickly veiled from his sight. Sulai had obviously warned her that any further show of disobedience would be harshly dealt with. He had won the first round!

Beneath the show of docility there was still fire, and that pleased him. A lesser, more cautious, man might have hesitated to rouse it in her, but Nicholas Benedict was not a man to shy away from a challenge; besides, she would be of no use to him without spirit.

There was no denying she had the bearing of a woman of breeding, he acknowledged, as she seated herself opposite him at the table. Even as he first saw her, in shackles, dirty and unkempt, there was an air of superiority about her, a pride that put her apart from the other women. A lady turned whore, if he was to believe what he had been told—and he had no reason not to. His own enquiries from officers and men aboard the prison ship had borne out what Captain Grayson had told him; that she was a hellion, a troublemaker, whose morals left much to be desired. All that and the face of an angel of innocence, protesting that her virtue and good name had been abused. He cared little what she had once been. He had bought her for a purpose, and, so long as she fulfilled her duties as he ordered, then she, too, would be allowed to forget it. If that was what she wanted.

He had been surprised that Sulai had been unable to get much information from her. A young girl, after months at sea in hellish conditions, should have been eager for the companionship of another woman, yet Celina MacNeill was not. Neither had she made any great fuss over the new clothes she had been given. A great improvement on the grey calico, he thought, allowing his gaze to dwell on the slender body beneath the lilac silk. The colour made those lovely eyes appear even darker in the flickering candlelight. What thoughts lurked behind that even gaze? He knew she was afraid of him, but she hid it well, as if it had become an accomplished art. Like the entertaining of seamen below decks in order to obtain another morsel of food. She did not look capable of sinking to such a level.

'No.' Celina's hand covered the glass in front of her as Xavier bent to fill it with wine from the decanter he held. 'I will have nothing to drink.'

'You will,' Nicholas said tersely, 'unless you want to be taken down to the hold, and to spend the days there until we reach Jamaica, where I shall sell you immediately. You are accustomed to the company of rats, I believe?'

Celina's cheeks were suddenly ashen. His twin-barbed remark had been intended to hurt her, and it did, but he had no way of knowing which hurt her most. The taunt that she had given herself to any man who fancied her for an extra crumb of food, or his reference to the weeks she had spent in solitary confinement in a damp, dark cell with only the rats for company?

'You know?' Her voice was hardly audible. Was she to

be spared no humiliation even now?

'I made enquiries as to why you were the only woman still in chains. You gave the first officer quite a few scratches, I believe. Not that you got off lightly yourself!'

'As I will anyone who dares to try and force themselves on me like an animal,' Celina flung back, stung by the injustice of his remarks. He thought the worst of her, that was clear. He knew nothing and she would tell him nothing.

Nicholas watched a flicker of indecision cross her face and for a moment thought she was about to tell him how wrong his suspicions were, but she relapsed into silence and he felt unreasonable anger stir inside him. Damn the girl, why did she not defend herself? Did she not care that her reputation was in shreds?

'As I told you before, I answer to no one for my actions. You will have seven years to grow used to my ways, Celina,' he laughed softly. As the implication behind his words sank into her, he watched her eyes grow wide and her fingers curled tightly round the linen napkin which lay on the table.

'I am sure you will tire of me long before then.'

'You will not find what I have in mind for you at all unpleasant. Fill her glass, Xavier, and let us eat. I have had only a light meal prepared for us, nothing you will find indigestible after months of meagre diet.'

Light! There was lobster, freshly caught that morning, and crayfish, accompanied by several kinds of sauces. Fresh salad and vegetables and fruit in abundance. The negro called Xavier served them and then retired into the background, but the moment she touched her wine, the glass was refilled. He was going to get her drunk, Celina thought in horror. He had made his intentions towards her only too clear. She belonged to him until he tired of her and sold her again. She would never accept it, but what else could she do? Friendless and in a strange country, without money, without freedom—she was helpless. How she wished she could resist the delicious food placed before her, but she had learned what it was like to be half-starved. She never wanted to be that way again. There was a smile on the face of her companion as he watched her eat. In accepting what he offered her—the food and the clothes—she was also accepting the fact she was his property. She hated him for that.

She looked across the table into the bronzed face, and asked quietly, 'Jamaica, is that where I am going?'

'It is my home. Yours, now, for a few years anyway.' Xavier served her port, and brandy for Captain Benedict. She made no attempt to touch it. Her head was already spinning from the sweet wine she had consumed with the lobster. Such privileges for a mere servant-girl? No, he had other plans for her! 'You will like it. I own a tobacco plantation some miles inland. The forest round the house is full of beautiful flowers, and you might walk there if you wish. You will have plenty of spare time to do so. Perhaps it will remind you of home.'

'Only the sound of the sea can do that.' Celina spoke without thinking, and immediately he seized upon her words, aware that, where the wine had failed, talk of home might have loosened her tongue. She guarded it well, he gave her that.

'Your home was near the sea?' he prompted.

'On a headland, where the waves danced over the bay below and the seagulls wheeled and screamed over the house. Such a beautiful house . . . once.'

'It is gone?' How wistful her eyes became when she spoke, he noticed.

'English troopers burned it after they had . . . They burned it,' she repeated dully. 'The English have deprived me of everything.'

'You would do well not to regard me in the same light, Mistress. I would not take kindly to that,' Nicholas paused in the act of lighting a cheroot and considered her with narrowed gaze.

'The soldiers destroyed my home, took my family from me. You have taken the last thing I had left—my freedom. I see little difference between you,' Celina retorted.

He knew what was in her mind, what had been ever since he had first seen her on the quay and then had reappeared to buy her. He could have told her how mistaken she was, but she had roused the devil in him and he drew deeply on his cheroot. His silence, and the way he considered her boldly, confirmed her fears.

'You have until we reach land again, which will be a few days only, to change your attitude,' he remarked at last, and saw her stiffen defiantly. He had not intended the wine to give her courage, only to make her more willing to answer his questions. Before they reached Jamaica he had to be sure he had not made a mistake. 'Go to bed, you foolish child, before you make me very angry. You would not like to see me angry, Celina. I have been told I look half-way between the devil and the ghost of Blackbeard. Having never seen either, I cannot comment on the resemblance.'

She should have been accustomed after all this time to being told what to do in that tone of voice, but deep in her heart she had never accepted that she, Celina Mac-Neill, should have to take orders from anyone. She had been used to giving them, having servants to wait on her, to carry out her every wish. That had been in another life, she thought sadly, rising to her feet. But at least he knew now that she was not willing to go to his bed and would not easily accept his domination, even though in the end, she knew, she would be forced to submit to it. She had so many other torments.

'Think well on what I have said,' Nicholas murmured as she reached the door which Xavier was holding open for her. 'I shall have no trouble in selling you again in Jamaica, especially if I offer you in that dress. You could attract quite a number of prospective buyers, someone more to your fancy, perhaps, who would give you a fine carriage and set you up in some little house in the town and visit you several nights a week, hoping his wife never finds out. I am offering you more. I am offering you self-respect and dignity.'

If he expected an answer, he did not receive one. Celina hurried back to her own cabin without a backward glance.

Self-respect and dignity—at a price! She saw little difference between being installed in a town house or one in the country. 'I own a tobacco plantation some miles inland,' he had told her, and that was where he was taking her!

Some while later Sulai found Celina prostrate across the bed, her shoulders heaving with huge sobs. 'What is it, child? Are you feeling unwell? Have you eaten too much? I knew he shouldn't have given you such rich food so soon, but he wanted to make you feel . . .'

'Feel what?' Celina asked, raising a tear-streaked face. 'The food and the clothes—am I supposed to show him gratitude?'

'Do you think it out of place to do so?' the woman

asked, sitting alongside her on the bed. 'Do you prefer shackles and filthy clothes, and food which barely keeps you alive?'

'Of course not.'

'Did he touch you?'

'No! Why do you ask that? Did you expect him to? It is why he bought me, after all.'

'It is the only thing I could imagine that would make you so distraught.' Sulai produced a handkerchief and dried the girl's cheeks. 'You will see things in a different light when we reach the plantation. It is a beautiful house, with nice people who will want to be your friends. Little Marianna will welcome someone of her own age to talk to. That poor girl is starved of company.'

'Is—is she an indentured servant too?' Celina asked, sitting up. A smile touched Sulai's face as she instinctively smoothed down the folds of her skirts and pushed the hair back from her face.

'Good heavens no, child. She's the captain's sister. Much younger than he. That's why he bought you, to be her companion. She has no one but a no-good husband who barely gives her the time of day when the captain's not around.'

'Companion!' A small cry escaped Celina's lips and her hands flew to her flushed cheeks. 'You will not find what I have in mind for you at all unpleasant,' he had said. A companion, but not his! The inhuman monster— to have allowed her to believe otherwise! He had deliberately, cruelly, deceived her, allowed her to suffer the agony of her own thoughts all through dinner.

'If you want to get on with the captain, child, you will have to learn to trust him. I know it will be difficult for you at first, but you must make an effort, otherwise you will make life difficult for yourself,' Sulai warned in a gentle tone. 'Jamaica will be your home now, Nicholas Benedict will control your life. Accept it and he will not enforce any rigid rules, but he is not a man to be disobeyed.'

'Shall I like this plantation? He said there were forests and flowers.'

'Hundreds of wild ones, orchids and lilies and convolvulus. You can walk for miles behind the house, right up to the cliffs which overlook the bay, and there's a path down to the beach.'

'The house is near the sea?' Celina asked, suddenly interested.

'An hour away, maybe, but you'll see it all for yourself soon. So no more tears, eh?'

'You must think me very silly.'

'You are lonely and frightened, but now you have no need to be either. Sulai will always be your friend, and, although he might look like a fire-breathing dragon, Xavier is a good man. He is the captain's right hand and will do anything for him, so if you cross one, you cross the other. Don't do either, is my advice. You are still flushed, child. Why don't you get some fresh air before you go to bed? The night breezes in these parts are warm and pleasant. I'll stay until you return, if you like.'

'No, I shall be all right. Thank you, Sulai, you are being very kind and patient with me.' Celina slid from the bed. The cool night air might well relieve the nagging ache in her head. The wine, of course, and the tension that had been building up inside her ever since she had been brought aboard. A walk on deck would soothe her jangled nerves, and she would sleep better.

A full moon bathed the wooden decks in a silvery carpet. She paused for a moment at the top of the stairs, listening to the sounds that a ship makes in the night.

The sound of the waves against her bows, the sails billowing in the wind, the rigging creaking. The murmur of voices somewhere in the shadows from the sailors on watch. She stepped to the rail and leaned against it, feeling the breeze toss her loose hair about her shoulders, caress her flushed cheeks and slowly soothe and calm her wildly beating heart. She could hardly believe her good fortune. A companion to some young girl, as lonely as she was by the sound of it, despite the husband she possessed, living in a grand house in what were described as idyllic surroundings. Near to the sea. How wonderful.

She leaned her head against the rigging beside her and closed her eyes. Sulai was right. It was time to put the past out of her mind and accept her new future. A far brighter future than she had envisaged for herself while confined in the punishment cell—cold, dirty, in fear for her life. A new life in a new land. For her own peace of mind she had to accept it without reservations.

She caught her breath as she heard the scrape of a tinder-box close by, and her startled gaze encountered the shadowed features of Nicholas Benedict.

'Did I frighten you? I thought perhaps you might have been expecting someone.' After a moment he stepped towards her, a long cheroot between his lips. 'Are you not tired after your day's adventures?'

'I would hardly call them that, and I . . . I merely wanted some air,' Celina replied, fighting down the urge to resort to sarcasm. 'Why are you determined to think the worst of me, Captain Benedict?'

'My dear girl, from what I have seen of you so far, it is my estimation that any man who doesn't take a fancy to you is a damned fool. Or blind. I am neither, but then I have been forewarned by Grayson. That dress doesn't change the person wearing it, it merely makes her more attractive. I dare say, when my back is turned, my crew have no more scruples than those men aboard the prison ship. You have made it quite clear you intend to fight me all the way, so why should I not suspect you of trying to persuade one of the crew to help you to run away when we reach Kingston? What you could offer as payment would be most acceptable, I am sure.'

The tip of the cheroot glowed red in the darkness. He moved closer and she saw a smile on his face, illuminated by the moon. He was being deliberately provocative. She wanted to slap him.

'Have I spoiled things for you by coming on deck?' he mocked.

'No! There is no one. I wasn't . . . Oh, you are impossible! All evening you have made me think the worst of you, deliberately, as though you wanted to hurt me. What have I ever done to you that you should misuse me so? Why did you not tell me I was to be your sister's companion instead of—of . . .'

'My mistress? Sulai told you, then. I thought she would.'

'You should have told me,' Celina insisted, stung by his callousness. 'You were playing with me like a—a cat with a trapped mouse.'

'Is that how you feel? Trapped?' he asked softly. The wind caught her hair and whipped it in wild profusion about her face. Strands of it touched his cheek also for a brief moment before she swept it back.

She wished he would not stand so close, their bodies were almost touching with the swaying motion of the vessel, and his nearness was beginning to have a strange effect on her. She watched him toss away his half-smoked cheroot, forced her gaze to return to his face and the eyes which had never left hers. She began to realise in the continuing silence exactly what it was she had been assuming. She, Celina MacNeill, in her tight-fitting calico dress and bare feet had had something to offer this man, who was obviously rich and respectable and handsome enough to have any woman he chose—any beautiful, elegantly-gowned woman from among his own circle of friends. If he wanted the satisfaction of a servant-girl, he had no need to buy one! She had presumed too much in her fear and he had been right to act as he did.

'You will not feel trapped at Paraíso,' he said, and his voice was full of pride as he spoke, betraying a deep love of his home. 'You will have your own rooms and a servant to wait on you. All you want, in fact. All I expect from you in return is that you care for my sister. We shall go into more details later. You have much to learn about her.'

'And you, it seems,' Celina answered, glad he could not see the ashamed colour in her cheeks. 'I apologise for everything I have said and thought about you. You did not deserve it.'

'Did I not? Are you not again presuming too much? To know me, just because you have been proved wrong on one little matter?'

'If you are not prepared to accept my apology, I quite understand.' Celina stepped away from him. He was still angry with her. Perhaps tomorrow the hostile feeling would have diminished. 'Goodnight, Captain Benedict.'

Celina did not know whether what happened next was the fault of the ship or the giddiness in her head from the wine she had drunk, but she stumbled and would have fallen, had strong arms not enfolded her.

'Too much wine, or has the touch of silk persuaded

the real Celina MacNeill to come forth from hiding?'
Nicholas's voice in her ear had a sudden hardness about
it she found frightening. She tried to free herself, but was
caught in a tight embrace. 'Let's find out, shall we?'

She threw back her head, her mouth opening to
protest at the indignity of being held so close against him
that she could hardly breathe. His mouth descended on
hers before she could utter a word, shocking her into
silence. She could not remember the last time she had
been kissed by any man other than her brother. She had
never entertained serious feelings for anyone, even
though she had been courted by several eligible young
men, all approved by her parents. Young red-haired Ian
Fraser, she remembered, and Michael MacNeill, son of
her father's best friend, but none of them had roused the
slightest passion in her and she had regarded them only
as close friends.

She wriggled and writhed in his hold, panting beneath
the lips which ground into hers, forcing them apart,
taking them by storm. Dear God, could she have been so
wrong? What if Sulai had lied to her to make her more
responsive to his advances? It had worked. She had been
totally unprepared for this and, still weak from the long
months of confinement, was no match for his strength.

Her limited powers gave out. Helpless, tearful, she
was aware of him raising his head and looking down into
her face. When she instantly tried to avert her head, he
wound a lock of her loose hair round his fist and held her
fast again.

'That's better. Given up play-acting at last, have you?
Let's see what we really have beneath the façade, shall
we.'

His lips took hers again and she was forced to endure
the long-drawn-out kisses pressed on her bruised mouth.

Kisses which made her senses reel. No man had ever touched her in this manner before. It outraged her, and yet at the same time there was an element of excitement about the way his hard body pressed hers back against the rail, the touch of his hand moving over her bare shoulder, the whispered endearments which came between the kisses.

She felt like a tiny boat being tossed about on a rough sea at the height of a storm against which she had no defence. Huge waves threatened to wash over her, to drag her down into the depths of the ocean where she would remain for ever. It was wrong, but she did not want Nicholas Benedict to release her. A soft moan of despair broke from her lips. She grew limp in his grasp and, without realising it, her lips gave him answer.

'Now I understand why the first officer was so willing to risk the displeasure of his captain,' Nicholas said, suddenly thrusting her from him. She clung to the rail to steady herself. A contemptuous twist deepened his mouth as he stared at her, adding coldly, 'I shall have no further need of you tonight, Mistress MacNeill. Go to bed.'

Celina turned and stumbled away from him, with tears streaming down over her cheeks. She did not care if he saw them. Her bright future had been destroyed. He had meant none of it. She undressed in her cabin and crawled into bed, heedless of what lay ahead.

'The last two days he's been going to take her ashore in Kingston and sell her again,' Xavier remarked dourly, and Sulai looked up in surprise from the blouse she was sewing. 'Now he's changed his mind again.'

'You believed him? He'll never get rid of that girl. Mark my words. He'll never let her go.'

'You talk nonsense, woman, like always. Where is she?'

'In her cabin, same as always. Hasn't stirred out of it for days.'

'The captain says to make sure you keep an eye on her. She's not to get near the gangplank.'

'She won't,' Sulai promised him, and he left her to rejoin Nicholas Benedict on deck, annoyed by the knowing smile always on her face whenever she spoke of Celina. What did she know that he did not, he thought? Nothing. Woman's fancies, that's all it was.

'Where is she?' Nicholas addressed the same question to him the moment he appeared. His expression was unreadable.

'In her cabin,' Xavier replied. 'Sulai will watch her.'

'When you get back, take over from her, she has to do some shopping.' Nicholas paused, his gaze sweeping along the deck to the hatchway, but then the arrival of a carriage on the quayside diverted his attention and all thought of Celina vanished from his mind as he went to meet the woman waiting for him.

From the open window in her cabin, Celina watched him go, saw the slender, dark-haired woman who alighted and came to greet him, felt herself colour as she watched them kiss. Days had passed since that night, but it was still vividly clear in her mind. She had not gone on deck since then. To stay below was no great hardship, she was used to it, and this time it was at least in some degree of comfort. And there was Sulai to talk to. At first she had refused to speak to her at all, but eventually the woman had convinced her there had been no deception on either her part or that of Nicholas Benedict. The plantation called Paraíso did exist, and so did his sister. She *was* to be her companion. At least that had been his

intention. Celina knew by the hesitation in Sulai's voice
that Nicholas Benedict was having second thoughts.
Was she to be sold again here in Kingston?

Why had he treated her in such a brutal fashion if her
suspicions had been so unfounded? She had no answer
to that question. Only the words he had spoken to her on
deck before he had seized her in his arms and ignited a
flame in her heart she knew would never die. 'It is my
estimation that any man who doesn't take a fancy to you
is a damned fool.' By his own admission he was not a
fool. Was it possible he had bought her with the best of
intentions, yet found himself attracted to her even so?
No, of course not. She was deluding herself again. A kiss
meant nothing to a man. He had probably kissed a dozen
servant-wenches the same way and not given it a second
thought.

'What am I to do with you?' Sulai declared in exasperation, when she returned from her shopping ex-
pedition laden down with parcels and packages and
found Celina lying on her bed exactly as she had left her
four hours before. 'And what do you think you will
achieve by not eating? You've not touched your lunch.'

'I'm not hungry. Is he back yet? I have to know what is
going to happen to me. If he is going to sell me . . .' Her
lips trembled at the thought, and instantly the woman
was at her side, tossing several parcels down beside her.

'Open them. See what I have brought you.'

Hope rose in Celina's eyes. She snatched up one and
tore the paper from it. Two pairs of leather shoes. One
pair dark green, the other blue.

'I've ordered more. Now the other ones.' Sulai
laughed and ripped open another, and Celina gasped at
the bolt of material she held and tentatively reached out
and touched the delicate fabric. White brocade, inter-

woven with silver thread. Sulai enthused, 'Against that hair, it will be stunning. I've another bolt for day dresses, but this was my best buy. It will make a beautiful ball-gown, perhaps two. Mistress Marianna's own dressmaker will be coming to the plantation next week. By the end of a month you will have a whole new wardrobe, child. Doesn't that please you?'

'Brocade, like this, for a companion, Sulai?' Celina asked meaningfully, and the woman frowned in annoyance.

'Paraíso is not a prison. Do I look as if he puts shackles on me at night? No one wears chains there unless it is of his, or her, own choosing. Every place has troublemakers—we are no different and the captain knows how to deal with them—but for the rest of us . . . Good heavens, child, I don't know what's in his mind, why he should want to dress you like a fine lady, except perhaps that a companion to his sister is a position of importance, and you must look the part. I've another dress for you, to match those blue shoes, too,' she added, as Celina continued to stare at the parcels strewn around the room. 'Open the rest of them while I go and have some food heated up for you and no arguments. You'll eat it.'

'Xavier says you can go on deck for a while.' Sulai stood in the doorway, staring across to where Celina sat at the table. The tray before her was empty and the woman gave a nod of satisfaction. 'The captain is still ashore,' she added, and Celina rose to her feet with a grateful smile for the extra information. Sulai's purchases had overwhelmed her. Everything she might need: underclothes, stockings, shoes, a new dress, the exquisite bolts of cloth, and the little essentials only another woman would think of. 'You won't do anything silly, will you? There's a guard on the gangplank.'

'No, nothing silly.' Celina had long since given up that wild idea, and the way the man moved to block the route of escape, as she appeared on deck, told her she would not be allowed past him. Most of the crew who had gone ashore earlier had returned, and she watched preparations for the ship to get under way again as soon as Nicholas Benedict returned. He would not be too anxious to do that with such an attractive companion, she mused.

The same carriage brought him back towards seven o'clock. The woman alighted as before and walked a little way to the ship with him. Her skin was flawless, Celina saw, the red mouth full and sensuous. She raised a jewelled hand to the cheek of the man beside her, drew his head down to hers and kissed him, careless of the grinning faces that appeared at the rail to watch her, and disappeared in an instant as Nicholas turned to come aboard.

'Is everything ready, Mr Harris?' The first mate was waiting for him for last-minute instructions. 'Good. Let's go home, then.'

At first Celina thought he had not seen her, for he strode across the deck without looking once in her direction, but as he reached the open hatchway, he turned, his eyes directly on her face.

'Come below, I want to talk to you,' he ordered.

Full of apprehension, she slowly followed him to his cabin. Whatever he was about to tell her, she would show no outward signs of relief or, if the news was bad, despair. She had survived transportation only because she had withdrawn into herself, allowed no one to come near her thoughts, to invade the singular world she wove around herself. Nicholas Benedict had drawn her from that world, brought her back to life with his barbed remarks, his deliberate attempts to taunt her, and she had suffered dearly for it. No more. He would not reach her again!

'Sit down, Celina.' She perched herself on the edge of a chair and watched him remove his jacket and toss it across another chair beside him. He poured himself some brandy and turned back to her, leaning against the large mahogany desk which dominated the room. There was no friendliness in his eyes or in his voice as he said, 'I was of a mind to get rid of you, do you know that?'

'I—I guessed. Why did you not do so?'

'My reasons are not your concern.' He had held a woman in his arms that night whose body and kisses had promised much, yet he had sensed something lacking— or missing—in the response he had forced from her. Had she stumbled, drunk too much wine? Or was he blind not to heed Grayson's warning? Was his sister and her needs merely an excuse to keep this girl, whose sad eyes had haunted him since that first day on the quay at Antigua? If she was being maligned by his thoughts, then time would be on her side for her to prove otherwise. On his, too, if she were indeed practising a deception. Either way, the advantage would be his. 'Tomorrow we will reach Paraíso. Are you prepared for that? Will you do whatever I tell you to do?'

'I have no choice,' Celina answered, and met his searching gaze without flinching. 'Yes, Captain Benedict, I will do what I am told.'

'I'm glad to see the things Sulai purchased for you have made you realise how comfortable life will be if you are sensible.' He had not expected capitulation so completely, and the words came across the room at her like a whiplash. There was no reaction. She sat and looked at him and said not a word. 'When we reach the house, I

will introduce you to my sister, Marianna. She is nineteen and has been married for one year. Her husband . . . he is of no importance. You will see what I
mean when you meet him. Always remember he is her
husband. There will be men enough for you on the
plantation if you crave attention.'

Only with an effort did Celina hold her tongue.
Nicholas stared at her, angry lights flickering in the
depths of his eyes at her silence, then, putting aside his
glass, he relaxed into a chair and crossed his long legs.
'At last I think we begin to understand each other,' he
murmured. He was pleased she had not risen to his jibes,
she realised. Never! Whatever she felt, he would never
know it.

'Marianna is a cripple. An accident, only a short while
after she and Jean were married. She has never been the
same since, in her outlook on life, I mean. Once she was
the most lively, spirited girl in Jamaica. A veritable
tomboy for all her fine clothes and we were close . . .' He
broke off with a frown.

'I'm sorry,' Celina said simply. She felt for the poor
unfortunate girl, to be deprived of life so young. In a way
they were alike. Nicholas's eyes gleamed at her reply.

'You will not be at Paraíso for that.'

'For what?' She looked at him, not understanding.

'To pity her. She's had enough pity and sympathetic
words from people who don't give a damn. She needs a
crutch, someone to lean on. You, Celina. One cripple
helping another. One of you may emerge a whole person
again.'

'I don't know what you mean?' It was as if he had read
her mind.

'You need help as much as she does. Another chance
at life. It's available for you both; all you have to do is

reach out and grasp it with both hands. I want Marianna to start taking an interest in things again, to get out of bed more, go for carriage-rides, begin receiving people at the house again. After all, she is mistress there. She does none of these things.'

'But her husband,' Celina protested in puzzlement. 'A bride of one year . . . are they not close?'

'He is most attentive to her, within my sight. He is my overseer. He has little time to spend with her. You will spend all your time with her, persuade her back to life again.'

'And if I cannot bring about this miracle?' He spoke with affection of his sister, yet it seemed he deprived her of her husband's company.

'Your very existance at Paraíso depends on it, Celina.' Nicholas swallowed his brandy and stared at her over the rim of his glass. She had grown pale, but was still in full control of herself. What had happened in the few short hours he had been away to change her so? The eyes were as listless as when he had first seen her, the pale face expressionless. Where was the fire he had felt when he held her in his arms, the anger usually flung back at him when he began an assassination of her character?

'Then I must achieve success, must I not?' She rose to her feet. 'May I go now?'

He nodded and she left him. When Xavier came to enquire if he required supper, Nicholas was still sitting where she had left him, the empty glass unnoticed in his hand. The question was asked twice before he even responded, and the fierce frown between his brows still remained, as he rose and refilled his glass.

Sulai gave a husky laugh as she lay by Xavier's side in her cabin that night. She was always more relaxed whenever she was away from Paraíso, Xavier realised, and did not know why. She loved it as much as he did. Soon he would ask Captain Benedict to allow them to marry, but he would say nothing to her until it was all arranged.

'Did I not tell you he wouldn't let her go?' She turned and laid her cheek against his shoulder, and her liquid brown eyes were content with the aftermath of making love. One day, perhaps, she would be able to tell this man she loved of her feelings, her dreams. 'They were meant for each other. As we are. Celina will never leave Paraíso.'

CHAPTER
THREE

DESPITE THE reserved attitude she continued to show before Nicholas Benedict, Celina could not help feeling excitement rising inside her as the ship slid into a pleasant little bay the following morning and dropped anchor. Sulai had talked continuously of the house and Marianna, arousing her curiosity more and more as the hours passed. All she had to do was to care for Marianna and be civil to her brother. Neither were great hardships after what she had endured for the past two years. In return she would have a comfortable home, clothes and food. Free to do as she pleased within the confines of the Paraíso plantation, but not beyond its boundaries. In time, perhaps, some miracle would happen to change that, and time was all she had.

Another chance at life was how Nicholas had described it. She would accept the opportunity which had come her way, and learn to live again, but in her own way. She would keep her own counsel and allow no one to breach her defensive barricades. As she had managed it once before under the most difficult of circumstances, so she would again, thus making her life pleasant and uncomplicated—and safe!

'The captain's waiting for you on deck,' Sulai told her as she sat in the window-seat watching the unloading of casks and sacks. She had put on the new blue dress and matching shoes and tied her hair back with some ribbon Sulai had bought in Kingston. She looked as serene as an angel, the woman thought as she collected together Celina's belongings, yet she was deeply troubled. Every night since she had come aboard she had tossed and turned in the throes of some hideous nightmare which caused her to call out in terror. Each time Sulai had come to her and comforted her until she fell asleep again. It was not mentioned between them. When the time was right for it to be brought out into the open, Sulai would listen.

She had told Nicholas about it the second time it had happened, and tried hard to recall the strange-sounding names Celina had called out, succeeding with only one.

'Coloden,' she said, with a shrug of brown shoulders. 'At least that's what it sounded like to me.'

'Culloden!' Nicholas looked startled. 'My God, what was she doing there? It was a bloodbath, and afterwards, too, so I've heard. English soldiers went on to the battlefield for days, bayoneting the wounded to death.'

'It was as though she were looking for someone. She calls him "Davie". Her man, maybe.'

'Maybe.' The man she had lost in war and sought in the arms of common seamen and the like, perhaps. It would go partially towards redeeming her wantonness of character to have had such a reason, he thought. Sulai's words came back to him as Celina came on deck, picking up her skirts to avoid the cargo strewn around. 'Who was Davie?' he asked, as she came up to him, and the violet eyes widened with the unexpected shock, then quickly looked away towards the beach.

As she answered, her tone told him that she had drawn a curtain over that part of her life and would open it for no one, least of all for him. 'A friend.' She could

have told him the truth, but that would have led to more
questions and inevitably pain. She had done with both.
It was none of his concern anyway. David was her
memory, not to be sullied by speaking of him to this man
who valued human life at no higher than ten pounds.

'Killed at Culloden?' Nicholas pointed towards the
shore, and she saw a longboat start back towards them.

'Yes. Am I allowed to keep no secrets, Captain
Benedict?'

'Sulai has told me of your nightmares. I thought it
might help you to talk about them,' he replied casually.

'Time will heal what ails me,' Celina said quietly.
'And I have seven years, have I not?' She looked beyond
the boat heading towards them, and the stretch of
golden beach, to the cliffs and the house just visible at
the top of them, like a lonely sentinel keeping constant
vigil on the bay below. Benedict's Bay, Sulai had told
her it was called, named by Nicholas's father on his first
visit. 'Is that the house?' She would be able to hear the
sound of the sea from her room.

'No, that's the place my father built for my mother.
It's not lived in now, not since she died. The new house is
about a mile further inland. Built for my stepmother.
She's dead, too, and my father travels a great deal. You
may meet him one day.' Again he seemed to have the
ability to read her thoughts. 'Only Marianna and I and
her husband live at the house now, apart from the
servants, but we once entertained quite often. The
house was never empty. Perhaps, if you can do something with my sister, it will live again. It's been a long
time since Paraíso has welcomed people beneath its
roof.'

Craig Tor had once known lavish balls, birthday
parties and Christmas celebrations when the huge old

beams echoed with laughter and music. Only 'Mac-
Neill's Lament' would be played among the silent stones
now, and the sounds of merriment would be hidden
inside the hearts of those who had once enjoyed its
hospitality.

Watching her, Nicholas saw the sadness which crept
into her expression. Memories again. He had them, too.
Some happy, some he could hardly bear to recall, which
came to him in the night, as hers did. But he could share
them with the most important person in his life, the only
other person in the world, apart from his sister, that he
cared for. Celina MacNeill had no one! One day, he
vowed, if it was the last thing he ever did, he would make
her open her heart to him.

The longboat took them to the beach, just the two of
them, and then returned for Xavier and Sulai and the
luggage. Nicholas looked round him as if expecting to
see another face, aside from the negroes and sailors
carrying the cargo to the cliff-top, and a flicker of
annoyance crossed his features when he found it absent.

'It's a long climb.' He looked up at the sheer rocks
above them. Large steps had been hacked from the face
to make it easier to ascend, but even so it was hard going,
as Celina saw from the men who passed her, their faces
wet with perspiration. He beckoned forward a young
negro boy. 'Take Bobo's hand. Hold it fast and don't let
go. I'll bring up the rear.'

Some ten minutes later Celina reached the top,
scarcely able to breathe. Tiny ringlets of damp hair clung
to her forehead and cheeks. She stood gulping in great
mouthfuls of air until Nicholas joined her. His jacket
was slung carelessly over one shoulder, his shirt-sleeves
were rolled back over sun-tanned arms where the blond
hair was bleached almost white. The arduous climb had

hardly winded him, she realised, as she bent to wipe the dust and sand from her shoes. Inches of it clung to the skirts of her dress, and she shook them with a frown.

A carriage was waiting some yards away, with a liveried driver. As Nicholas escorted her towards it, Celina looked around her in awe. The headland where Craig Tor had stood had been beautiful to her, but bleak. Here, at Paraíso, the grass beneath her feet was the greenest she had ever seen, and small yellow flowers pushed their way towards the sun in hundreds of tiny clusters to make a huge golden carpet. Ahead, the land dipped sharply beside the silent house, where untended flowers grew in profusion in the garden, and roses, some well over six feet in height, entwined together in a mass of red and pink blooms and filled the air with their rich perfume. A large iron gate, closed and barred, restricted entrance to the wildness beyond, the desolation that had once given pleasure to a woman. A few of the windows were heavily shuttered, but not all, she noticed. In places, the grass and weeds had been trampled aside as though someone did come here from time to time. The path to the gate was well-trodden, too. Did the man at her side make solitary visits to this house where, she suspected, he had been born?

I would not let such a place stay unlived-in, Celina thought as the carriage moved away, and she stared back at the veranda, its white paint peeling from the wooden supports, with a rocking-chair alongside the main doors. How she would have loved to sit there and listen to the sound of the sea, dwelling on those memories that were so dear to her. It would almost be like home again.

Tall, heavy trees suddenly obscured her view, and she was struck by an intense feeling of sadness as if in that short space of time the strange house had reached out in its loneliness and touched her, drawn her to it, offering her sanctuary within its walls. How foolish! It was just an old place, probably crawling with rats inside, and she was being silly.

The man-made road along which they were travelling was flanked on both sides by frangipani bushes. Thick clumps of vines, some in flower, were dotted between and occasionally there was a bright splash of magnificent red as they passed wild hibiscus. She could hear birds calling to each other amid the leafy branches. The trees were beginning to thin out slowly, giving way to open fields which stretched as far as she could see. There was an air of tranquillity about the place which calmed her wildly-beating heart, and she leaned forward in her seat a little more, enthralled by what she saw. Men and women, mostly coloured, were moving along the rows of plants, inspecting the huge leaves which were at least two feet in length and half as wide. In another field cutting had begun and, as he saw it, Nicholas too moved to the edge of his seat, his gaze scrutinising the procedure.

'September is the busiest month at Paraíso. The tobacco is ready for harvesting.' Obviously satisfied with what he saw, he sat back again. She felt his eyes on her questioningly. 'And what do you think of your first sight of your new home? Is it not pleasing to you?'

'It—looks very—nice.' She was hesitant with her answer, not wanting to sound either excited or enthusiastic at the prospect of living in these fabulous surroundings, and he gave an exclamation of annoyance.

'Nice! *Nice*, girl? It is paradise compared with what you have ever known. Come now, be honest and admit it.'

'I have never seen such beauty or smelt such sweet

fragrance in the air, but it cannot replace what I have lost. It is merely a substitute that I must bear until I am free to do otherwise,' she replied with great dignity. 'Nothing will ever take the place of the home I have lost.' Yet, even as she spoke, her thoughts were back along the path at the house which stood on the cliff.

'If this manner of yours is intended in some way to repay me for what happened the other night, let me warn you it will succeed only in angering me—as you did then,' Nicholas said curtly, irritated by the quiet hostility about her.

'Why do you think that, sir? Am I not your property to do with as you please? You have doubtless kissed many other servant-girls without one scrap of regard for their feelings, so why should you consider mine?'

She was voicing what had been uppermost in her mind since it happened, and saw a lazy smile play around the lean mouth, to confirm that she was correct.

'Indeed I have, but not many of them expected more from me.'

She gasped at the insult and, for a moment, as those violet eyes registered intense displeasure, he thought she might throw herself at him and tensed himself expectantly. Celina's hands were clenched tightly in her lap, and she fought against the urge to slap the smile from his face for daring to speak to her in such a way. She must continue to control the pride within her which leapt to the surface each time they were together. It amused him to taunt her, and he would cease only when he saw that she would not rise to his bait.

Averting her gaze, she stared stolidly out of the window until they reached the house, where more servants came hurrying out to help them both to alight and to remove the luggage so that the carriage could return to fetch the others.

'Xavier will introduce you to the servants later. Come, I shall introduce you to my sister now. The sooner you begin your duties and are fully occupied with some kind of work, the better,' Nicholas said tersely, and she followed him inside without a word.

Her first impression was one of coolness, rooms where shuttered windows kept out both the brilliant sunshine and the extreme heat. She could smell the scent of flowers, intermingled with that of polish, and noted how all the heavy wooden furniture glowed with a muted brilliance. She had not wanted to like the house, but merely to accept it, as she had truthfully said to her companion, as a substitute for the home lost to her. But as she followed Nicholas up a long, winding staircase of gleaming wood and marble dominated overhead by an enormous glass chandelier that must have held over a hundred candles, along carpeted corridors where black faces smiled and greeted not only the return of the master of Paraíso, but her arrival too, her resolve began to weaken. She wanted to belong again somewhere. Why not here?

She entered a room dark with shadows. The windows were shuttered, and the heavy velvet curtains were drawn. Nicholas strode across and flung them open, and was rewarded by an exasperated exclamation from the direction of the four-poster bed, where a young girl with bright red curls tumbling past her shoulders regarded him with some hostility. Surely this was not his sister Marianna, Celina thought in surprise. The girl she had come to care for? The pretty face became sullen as Nicholas approached the bed, shattering her illusion that they were close. It was the impression he had given her as he spoke of her needs, his hopes for her recovery.

'Oh, it's you. I thought it was Jean with my lunch,' came the ungracious remark, and Nicholas's eyes narrowed as, across the room, he caught Celina's intense scrutiny.

'I leave you for a few weeks and you go back to your old ways.' He bent over the bed and kissed the offered cheek. 'It's a lovely day. Why aren't you out in the garden with a book or thinking about a ride in the carriage? You promised me you would.'

The lion had been tamed by a child, Celina thought, watching them. His voice held no reproach for the fact he had found her still abed, or for the ungraciousness of his reception. She was his sister and he did love her, Celina realised. His Achilles heel—and in her charge!

'Where can I go? Whom can I talk to? Without you to work him so hard, Jean has spent more time with me while you were away, but he has the plantation to run . . . So little time for me, even then.'

'I have brought someone who will change all that. A companion. Come here, Celina. Come and meet your mistress,' he ordered, without turning round.

Celina moved to the edge of the bed and was inspected by a pair of alert blue eyes, so like those of her brother, yet lacking the intensity Celina found so disturbing. Every inch of her was thoroughly inspected, while she held her breath.

'Where did you find her? What's her name?'

Nicholas looked up, indicating with a slight motion of his head that Celina should supply the facts herself. He intended to make it as difficult for her as he could, she thought bitterly. Now he was repaying her for the words tossed at him earlier and once again he achieved his aim of wounding her. He was in a position to do so!

'My name is Celina MacNeill. Captain Benedict bought me in Antigua.'

'A convict? Nicholas, what are you thinking of to bring a woman like that into our house . . . ?'

'I am no convict,' Celina broke in sharply. 'I'm a MacNeill from Craig Tor on the island of South Uist. My family rose for Charles Stuart last year, and paid the penalty for his defeat. As I am doing now. I was sentenced to transportation, to be sold as an indentured servant because I sheltered fugitive Highlanders from the butchery of English soldiers. I am proud of what I did. I would do it again.'

'You poor thing. Oh, Nicholas, how could anyone be so—so heartless as to sell a—a woman for such a triviality. Has the government in England lost all sense of reason?'

'Your concern is most commendable,' Nicholas murmured with a smile, 'But you did not show any at all for poor Sulai when I brought her here four years ago and you learned she had been beaten and abused by her past two masters. Is there a difference?'

His sister looked at him as though he had taken leave of his senses.

'Indeed there is. Sulai is a slave and always has been. She was raised to expect little from life. Mistress MacNeill is—well, look at her! How can you regard her in the same light?'

'Nevertheless, I have bought her to be your companion. She is yours to do with as you please.' But I will always have the last word, his eyes told Celina as he looked at her. He said, 'You will find my sister Marianna has a soft heart. Do not let me hear of you taking advantage of it.'

'Nicholas, that sounded like a threat. Go away, you

will not impose your will on the poor thing as you do on everyone else in this house,' Marianna flashed with a sudden show of spirit that quite changed her from the sleepy, unreceptive girl Celina had first seen into someone to be reckoned with. She could hold her own against her brother if it came to a match, she decided. 'Find someone to bring my lunch, and something for Celina, too. I shall call her that because she is going to be my friend, not my servant.'

'She is to be your companion,' Nicholas returned, frowning at the suggestion. 'You are not to allow her to take liberties. She will, given the slightest chance, I promise you.'

'Nonsense, we shall have fun together. I don't want her to fetch and carry for me, there are plenty of other servants to do that. If you want me to get out more, and you are always on at me to do so, then Celina will come with me. I will take the rides you insist upon, perhaps starting next week when we know each other a little better. It will be so good to have someone to talk to.'

She had fallen into the trap Nicholas had laid for her, Celina realised. How clever he was at manipulating people, even his own sister. By insisting that Celina should be treated as a servant he had further aroused the sympathy Marianna felt for her plight, and she suspected a naturally rebellious nature had done the rest.

'You will have to eat alone now. Xavier will be here in a moment and I want him to acquaint Celina with the rest of the household. Then he must find her suitable accommodation. I thought a room upstairs.'

'Where Sulai is? Certainly not. There are plenty on this floor, near mine. You may select any room you wish, Celina. You have my permission.'

'I am sure Captain Benedict would prefer to do th

himself.' Celina was aware of those eyes on her, even though she did not glance in his direction. 'But thank you for the kind thought.'

'Oh dear, you are not going to be as meek as a lamb, too, like everyone else, are you?' Marianna declared. 'Even my husband is beginning to look like a piece of furniture. He never steps from his place. Nicholas sees to that.'

'Marianna,' Nicholas said. 'Don't. Not now. I've only just come back.'

'To your precious Paraíso, where you are absolute ruler and all the rest of us are at your beck and call. When you grow bored or lonely, you take yourself off to Kingston to see your mistress and never give a thought for me, lying here, crippled, alone . . .'

'I thought you said Jean was spending more time with you?' Nicholas's face was pale beneath its tan. 'Damn it, the plantation all but runs itself until this time of year. He has very little to do.'

'That's not the way I hear it. You've had him going over the ledgers again . . .'

'Because he had work to catch up on. He's neglected them for too long, and I needed figures before I went away. It's not my fault he's lazy. He can leave at any time.'

'You'd like that, wouldn't you? You didn't want me to marry him in the first place. It's all right for you to have your amusements, no matter who you hurt in the process, but when I wanted to find a little happiness, get away from this place and a father who loathed the sight of me . . .'

'Enough.' Nicholas towered over the bed, his eyes blazing, and she cowered back from him and was silent. Half-way between the devil and the ghost of Blackbeard! If he looked this way now, when someone he loved could make him angry, Celina thought she never wanted to witness what he would look like if roused by an enemy. 'If you wish to continue this discussion we shall do so when we are alone. We do not quarrel with strangers present. I shall come and see you again this afternoon. I want to ride out first and look the place over. The cutting has begun, I noticed.'

'Jean thought some of it was ready. You approve, I hope?' Marianna's voice was tinged with sarcasm, but it was ignored.

'He was perfectly right.' He bent to kiss his sister, and motioned Celina to follow him downstairs.

She did not notice Sulai until she had reached the bottom of the staircase. Nicholas, striding ahead, lost in his own thoughts, passed within a foot of the two figures in the alcove to one side and proceeded into another room. The woman was held fast by a man whose back was towards Celina. That he was well dressed was all she saw, as her footsteps faltered. He was forcing kisses on the face and shoulders of the woman he held. Sulai was like a statue, neither struggling nor responding, but the look on her face was one of contempt. Her cheeks flooding with colour as she remembered herself in Nicholas's embrace, Celina hurried after him. It was none of her business. She had enough to contend with.

Nicholas, seated behind a carved desk before open french windows, was deep in conversation with Xavier. Without speaking, he waved her to a chair and resumed his discussion. Master and servant. Celina gritted her teeth and sat down on a velvet chaise-longue with hanging tassels. It was several minutes before he gave her his attention.

'I have instructed Xavier to give you rooms as close to

my sister as possible,' he said. The negro put down a
silver tray on which were a decanter and a crystal glass
and then retired some feet away. Nicholas helped himself to the brandy and relaxed back in his chair, pushing
the doubts which still remained about her to the back of
his mind. Marianna was glad of the company of another
woman; in that respect Celina was of use. 'He will now
introduce you to the rest of the household before he
takes you upstairs. You have already been given a maid
who is taking care of the unpacking, so you can return to
my sister very shortly. You understand what is required
of you, Celina? What I require of you?'

'Yes.'

'Then you may go.'

'Before I am introduced to the new acquisition?' a
voice declared from the doorway. The man who advanced towards Celina was in his late twenties, she
surmised, lithe of step, handsome in a foppish way. The
light-coloured hair curling to his shoulders was tied back
in a *queue*. A fastidiously trimmed moustache hovered
an inch above thin petulant lips that belonged to the face
of a child, not of a grown man. With horror she saw that
the black leather breeches he wore were identical to
those of the man who had been outside in the alcove. It
was too much of a coincidence that there were two men
in the same house in the same breeches!

'Well, Nicholas, where did you find this delightful
little creature? Does your lady-love know you stray out
of her sight?'

'Mistress Celina MacNeill—Marianna's husband,
Jean Leclerc. You must forgive him his atrocious sense
of humour. I don't think much of it either, it makes me
realise why the French and English are always at war,'
Nicholas drawled.

'*Enchanté*, Mademoiselle.' Jean Leclerc bent low over Celina's hand and barely touched the fingers to his lips. Nicholas was not amused by the gesture, she noticed. His narrowed gaze was full on her as he waited for her response. '*Etes-vous la nouvelle maîtresse da la maison?*' His voice was low and not meant to carry to the man at the desk behind him. The eyes which considered her were as insulting as the suggestion.

'*Non*, Monsieur. *Je suis une servante simplement*,' she replied, and Jean Leclerc stepped back from her with a laugh.

'*Vous parlez français! Bien.* We shall be able to spend many enjoyable hours together if you can spare her from her duties, Nicholas.'

'I suggest you remember the wife waiting for you upstairs, Jean. This one is out of reach.'

'Yours?' The man turned and stared at Nicholas almost challengingly.

'Mine,' came the answer, and he shrugged his shoulders briefly.

'*Dommage.* I came to tell you that three fields have been cut already. I was sure you would be pleased with my progress.'

'I am. I shall look forward to the steady continuance of work,' Nicholas answered. He did not offer the other man a drink as he refilled his glass, and, after a moment, Jean gave a half-smile and sauntered from the room.

As Celina rose to follow, he said in a voice which belied great displeasure, 'You did not mention you spoke French.'

'You did not ask me, sir. I also write it and a little Latin. I am quite good at mathematics, too.' In telling him these things she gave nothing of importance away. She could have told him so many other intimate details which must surely have touched his hard heart, but she did not. Her future was his! The past hers alone!

'Men on South Uist are mainly fishermen, aren't they?'

'Most of them.'

'How, then, does the daughter of a fisherman speak and write French?' he demanded with a scowl. 'I mean to know, Celina. You are in no position to refuse me an answer. My methods for handling difficult slaves would not appeal to you. Do not learn of them first hand.'

What did it matter if he knew, she thought wearily. She was who she was, and no one could take that from her, not even Nicholas Benedict, who owned everything but her birthright. Her head tilted proudly as she looked at him, and he was struck by the silent haughtiness which hung in the air between them as she gave him his answer.

'My father was Malcolm, Laird of Craig Tor. My mother, Margaret MacDonald of Benbecula. You are looking at the last of our line, Captain Benedict. Celina MacNeill, your very obedient servant, sir.' And she swept down in a curtsy that would have delighted her old French nanny, who had once despaired of her pupil ever reaching perfection.

'Obedience is what I demand from you.' If her words had caused Nicholas the slightest shock, it did not show itself in his face. 'Xavier will take you upstairs now. Return to my sister as soon as you can and stay well away from Jean. You both have work to do.'

'If Mr Leclerc wishes to converse with me, I can hardly prevent that.'

'Give him no opportunity.'

'Perhaps you should have me watched to ensure I do not seduce him,' Celina flared bitterly, forgetful of all the promises she had made to herself. He had told Jean

Leclerc she was his property, and that was true, but it was the *way* he had said it which troubled her. If she was to be pestered by unwelcome attentions, they would come from him, not from Marianna's husband!

'If you don't watch your tongue, girl, I'll take a whip to you,' Nicholas growled, getting up from his chair. There was one on the wall beside him, a long leather plaited whip of some six feet, perhaps more. Did he use that on his poor, helpless slaves? With the devil's own mockery in his tone, he added, 'Run along Celina, before you see Blackbeard.'

'I find you a very strange person,' Marianna declared one morning as Celina was brushing her hair. She had taken over this task, along with many others usually performed by a maid, but she did not mind. She was happy, something she had thought never to be again, and content beyond her wildest dreams.

'Why is that?'

'You have been here three weeks, yet I know as little about you as the first day you stood in this room and told me my brother had bought you. I chatter non-stop and you listen, but when you speak, you tell me nothing. It is deliberate, isn't it, Celina? You don't want me to know anything about you—or is there something so bad in your past you are afraid it will affect our friendship? Something you are afraid Nicholas might discover, perhaps? However terrible, I won't allow him to sell you again. I love having you here. I feel a different person. To talk to another woman, to be able to discuss silly things that only we talk about—it is such bliss.'

She had changed, Celina thought, as she rearranged the pillows behind the girl's head and made her more comfortable. Where before she had lain in bed and read, perhaps, but done very little else, now she sewed, or they discussed fashions or Celina read to her. She would tell her how the flowers were blooming in the garden, and report on the progress of the tobacco harvest. She had begun to take more of an interest again in the running of the house. For the past week she had undertaken the supervising of the menus, which until then had been Sulai's job. She involved Celina too in the everyday problems of the house, which now began to be brought to her, reminding the latter of the year she had spent in control of Craig Tor while her father and brother were away and her mother was ill.

'Stop fiddling with those things this instant. Come and sit down and tell me about yourself before I die of curiosity. Or shall I ask my brother? He knows about you, doesn't he?'

'He thinks he does. He believes what he has been told, but it is not the truth,' Celina replied grave-faced as she sat down in a chair beside the bed. 'He thinks me a woman of easy virtue. No better than a whore.'

'You!' Marianna gasped. 'Oh, no, that isn't possible. Is he blind? I think there are times when he is. I've noticed how you change whenever he comes into my room. You withdraw into yourself in a most frightening way. I've noticed too how he tries to antagonise you as if to make you retaliate. He can be hateful at times. Arrogant and selfish.'

'But you love him,' Celina interposed quietly, and Marianna gave a nod.

'Don't tell him I said so. I have not yet forgiven him for working poor Jean so hard. Last night he went to bed after only ten minutes with me, he was so exhausted.'

And went straight upstairs to Sulai's room, Celina thought, wishing she had not seen the furtive figure heading towards the next floor. She was convinced he was being unfaithful to the unfortunate girl who was confined to bed, unable to walk or fulfil her part of the wedding bargain. Nicholas knew too, she suspected, from the words which had passed between them, but it was a well-kept secret from Marianna.

'Enough of me, you are distracting me again. Always you do this. Why does my brother think—think the worst of you? You have given him no cause since you have been here.'

'When I was brought ashore from the prison ship at Antigua, I was in chains,' Celina said with a sigh. 'He saw them on me, and when I was offered for sale he was told I was like that for having attacked the first officer who had tried to bring me water and food while I was locked in the punishment cell.'

'Is that true?' Marianna asked in an awed voice. Celina had never shown the slightest inclination to violence; indeed she seemed the most docile of creatures and rarely spoke unless she was spoken to.

'That I attacked him? Yes. He tried to rape me below decks. It was common practice for the seamen to take women for amusement, although the captain had forbidden it. I often thought he deliberately turned his back on what was happening. He despised us all. Dirty heathen Scots!' Celina shuddered, even though the windows were open and warm sunshine was flooding the room. She would never forget those fumbling hands, the ripping sound as her bodice was torn open, the hot mouth closing over hers, silencing her screams of terror. He had been bothering her since the first week at sea, watching her, offering inducements to be pleasant to him, but she had ignored him. It went on day after day, week after week. Four times he had followed her, attempted to detain her, and somehow she had evaded him and his evil intentions, but that last time . . .

'They dared to put you in chains like an animal because you defended your honour?' Marianna was disgusted. 'What manner of men were they?'

'A prison ship changes people. It is a different world. A terrifying world where only the strong survive. I never thought I would. He had forced me into a storeroom. There was a hook on the floor by some casks. I don't know how I managed to reach it. Suddenly it was in my hand and I was hitting him with it. Again and again, Dear God, the blood on his face! It was horrible . . . but he let me go. They took me away and chained me. He said I had enticed him below and that it had happened many times before. He bribed other members of the crew to say I had been with them also. One night he came down to my cell and beat me—badly.' The bruises had gone from her back now, but not the memory from her mind. The healing ointment Sulai smoothed daily into the skin of her chafed wrists was working a miracle. Soon the marks there would also have vanished, but when she looked at her wrists, she would always see them.

"You have not told my brother this? Why not? He should know.'

'It is not important that he does,' Celina insisted. 'I care not what he thinks of me.' Liar, a voice within her cried. It matters more to you each day.

'I shall tell him,' Marianna declared.

'No! Please don't. You know, and that is all that matters to me. I would not like to think you mistrusted me for any reason, or thought ill of me. You have been so kind to me.'

'Kind! I have done nothing. You have done everything for me. It is time I began to repay this new feeling of life you have given me, Celina. For the first time in nearly a year I don't want to stay in this miserable bed and allow everyone to wait on me. I want to do the things I used to before the accident. Oh, I know I can't walk, but Xavier can carry me downstairs and Nicholas bought me a wheelchair months ago which I refused to use. I shall now. We shall go out together. Would you like that? Beyond Paraíso, if you wish. You are my friend, not a servant, not a prisoner, and I will not have you treated as one. We are both going to throw off our shackles, Celina. You and I together.'

It was as Nicholas had predicted. He knew his sister so well, Celina thought, smiling into the excited face. Had it been only three short weeks that this friendship had existed? It seemed like years. Marianna was infecting her with her new vitality and she allowed herself to be drawn along with it. It was what she wanted—she needed. The past did not rise up to haunt her in the night as often as it did before, and her face was beginning to lose the strained, haunted look it possessed when Nicholas brought her to Paraíso.

She was beginning to fill out, too, he noticed as he came unannounced into the room and caught both girls convulsed with laughter. It had been a long time since he had heard his sister laugh. It pleased him beyond words. Celina, he had seen neither laugh nor really smile, and he wondered if it was beyond her. The sound of her laughter had the clearness of a mountain stream, the gaiety and innocence of a new-born lamb gambolling beside its mother, and he halted on the threshold to watch her.

Her dress was of deep indigo, trimmed with creamy lace. The black tresses were swept to the side of her head and down over one shoulder. They were so long that they reached almost to the trim waist. How they gleamed in the sunlight! Sulai's special treatment, he suspected. The woman had taken Celina under her wing like a mother hen, with good results.

For three weeks he had watched and waited for her to make a wrong move, to confirm the doubts already in his mind, but she performed her duties faultlessly, was civil to him—although sometimes he sensed only with a great effort—and the rest of the household liked her. One of them to a disturbing extent, he thought, remembering the way Jean had watched her walking in the gardens the day before. He had been on the veranda enjoying a brief moment of relaxation before he returned to work when he had seen her, and then Jean following some distance behind. When she stopped he had spoken to her and it had been several minutes before she continued on her way alone. An assignation—after his warning? Jean had entered the house without seeing him, the smile on his face telling Nicholas he was well pleased with the encounter.

Yet, when he looked at her now, her face alight with happiness, it was difficult to believe she could lie and cheat and deceive so effectively. A lady by family only, and in looks. But her heart, he was convinced, was that of a wanton.

CHAPTER
FOUR

'NICHOLAS, I didn't hear you come in,' Marianna declared, looking up and catching sight of the silent figure. He saw Celina's smile fade and the guarded expression return. She moved back from the bed as he approached, and his sister offered her cheek. 'Ugh! You smell of horses. Where have you been?'

'Working. More of the men have gone down with some sickness and can't stand. I've at least two dozen flat on their backs. The doctor's with them now, but he's as baffled as I am. Anyway, I've spent half the morning rearranging work schedules. I came up here looking for Jean.'

'He isn't here, why should he be? I thought you had come to see me, Nicholas!' She caught his hand and he sat down beside her with a surprised smile.

'What's all this? Affection? I was beginning to think I was no longer your favourite person. When I find Jean I certainly won't be . . .'

'Would you—would you be pleased if I came down to dinner tonight?' Marianna asked hesitantly. The thought of having someone carry her downstairs was repulsive, but she overcame her distaste. Celina was right, she had given up. She was only nineteen years old, she wanted to see the gardens again, the plantation, her friends in Kingston. For twelve long months she had been a recluse and it had soured her, made her a shrew to everyone she loved. Poor Nicholas, to him most of all she had been horrible. He would never understand the cruel words she had thrown in his face or why she had changed so drastically towards him since the accident, and she had lost the courage to tell him. To regain her brother, she must lose her husband. It was a choice she was not strong enough to make.

Celina was strong. She had survived her ordeal and made Marianna realise how little she herself had lost. The use of her legs, yes, but she still had a family and a home and friends. None of which she had acknowledged in a long time.

'Do you mean it?' Nicholas asked, his face immediately registering pleasure. 'Of course it would, little one, it's what I've been trying to get you to do for months.'

'Well, you can thank Celina for persuading me. She's convinced me that I'm an idiot to sit up here all day, missing everything that's going on. To hear her talk you would think this is the most wonderful place in the world and the most exciting. I can't remember it being either, but I am about to find out if you have changed that,' Marianna laughed softly. 'Send Xavier up here about nine.'

'No, the pleasure of carrying you will be all mine,' Nicholas replied. The blue eyes gleamed as they fastened on Celina. 'So I have you to thank.'

'That is not necessary. I am pleased you are satisfied with me,' Celina replied.

It was like a game between two children, Marianna thought as she looked at them. One playing the master, the other a servant—only, with Celina, it was no game to be enjoyed or provide amusement. Nicholas made her feel inferior, she suspected, or had threatened her with some awful punishment if she did not satisfy him in her duties. And he played the master well, too well. It was hateful of him to make her feel so uncomfortable.

She withdrew her hand from his, an angry frown creasing her brows.

'Why is it that whenever the two of you are together I sense a battle, but one never takes place?' she demanded. 'Celina is always different when you are here, and I don't like it.'

'You exaggerate,' Celina protested in embarrassment. 'Captain Benedict's presence merely reminds me of my place, which is easy to forget when you treat me not as a companion, but as a friend.'

'If you are going to act this way tonight, I shall not come down.' Marianna's lips deepened into a sulk, her moment of pleasure spoiled by her brother's refusal to relinquish the reins of authority even within the confines of her bedroom.

'As you wish.' Without attempting to persuade her, as Marianna thought he would, Nicholas rose to his feet and left them.

'Please, don't hurt him because of me,' Celina said anxiously. 'That's not fair. Think of the pleasure it will give your husband to see you at his side at dinner, of the pleasure you too will gain from the courageous effort. The first of many.' Jean would be the last person to be pleased by Marianna's appearance if it meant she would be more aware of his comings and goings around the plantation. Sulai was not the only woman he went to, Celina had discovered. She had been given a chatterbox of a maid, a little coloured girl of fifteen, whose mother and father worked in the kitchens. She knew every piece of gossip floating about Paraíso and related it in great detail. Celina did not stop her. It was a way of learning about the place and the people, and one man in particular. As yet, she had discovered nothing about him apart from the fact he had a mistress in Kingston, which she knew already and was, it seemed, common knowledge on the plantation.

'Oh, Celina, you put me to shame,' Marianna cried in a small voice. 'You did not give up, did you, and the way ahead was far harder for you. I think Nicholas is angry because I have made a friend of you and that is not why he brought you here, is it? He does not like people to act in a contrary fashion, but he should know me by now. As a child I used to be a wicked little monster, but we were so close then.'

'I do not think circumstances have altered that drastically.'

'They have. I cannot tell you why, I can tell no one. One day, perhaps. You see I too have my secrets, as Nicholas has his—as you have. Open my closets, show me some dresses. I only hope I can still get into them, I have put on so much weight.'

An hour later Celina left Marianna still unable to make up her mind between the three dresses spread out across the bed. She was in the happiest of moods, her mind too occupied with the adventure of getting out of bed to feel sorry that she was unable to walk downstairs, as she had once done, and make a grand entrance.

She went directly to the kitchen and informed Sulai there would be an extra place to set at dinner. She herself would eat in her room. The news set the whole place buzzing with excitement. Marianna did not realise how much she had been missed, Celina thought, as she made her way to Nicholas's study, hoping he had not gone out again.

The door was slightly open. He stood with his back to her, his hands thrust deep into the pockets of his riding-breeches. The air was heavy with tobacco-smoke, despite the open windows. On a table there was a tray containing a plate of food, untouched, and a decanter of wine, half-empty.

'Captain Benedict, may I speak with you a moment?'

He did not answer and she thought he had not heard her, but as she opened her mouth to ask the question again, he turned slowly and lit a fresh cheroot.

'Your sister has changed her mind. Will you please collect her at nine o'clock. I have told Sulai to set another place,' Celina said, wishing he would not stare at her so intently, as though he was searching for something in her face—or in her heart. That was for ever closed to him. To discover what lay dormant there would give him total power over her.

'Come in and close the door.'

With great reluctance she obeyed. She had been hoping to escape back upstairs without another of these confrontations, for she was sure that was what he intended. As if he was trying to wear her down, to break her spirit.

'Marianna is right, you know. Every time we are together we fight a battle, don't we, Celina? Only *I* can win, you realise that, don't you?'

He stood a few feet from her chair, eyes narrowed as he stared at her down-bent head. That servile attitude again which annoyed him beyond reason, for he knew it was a front, yet, try as he might, he could not force his way past it.

'I don't know what you mean.'

'Look at me, girl. You know damned well what I'm talking about. You've slipped very easily into place here, Celina. Too easily. Marianna is treating you like an old friend already.'

'Is that not what you wanted?' Celina looked up with a sigh, which did not escape his notice. 'Can I do no right in your eyes? Be her friend, you told me, bring her back to life. For the first time in months she wants to come down to dinner, to be with you and her husband as one of the family again. It pleases you, I know that. I saw the look on your face when she held your hand. Yet you are annoyed too. You distrust me, don't you? You always will. It is in your mind now that I will try in some way to use her affection, her kindness, for my own ends. She was right, you are blind! What can I do when you hold my papers of indentureship? I can be sold at any moment and she can do nothing. Don't you think I realise that?'

'You appear to have thought things out very carefully,' Nicholas said coldly. How indignant she looked as she spoke, as though the suspicions were not only unjust, but maligned a pure character. Yet in only three short weeks she had achieved nothing short of a miracle! 'Did Marianna really say I was blind?'

'She said you were close once, but not now. Not as it was. She seems to blame herself for what has happened—whatever it was.'

'She is not at fault,' Nicholas said quietly, almost to himself. 'She was too young to marry, so ignorant of many things she should have been told. And it was I who drove her to the mad decision to elope. I wanted only to protect her . . .' He broke off, aware that Celina was hanging on every word. 'Has Marianna spoken of her accident at all?'

'No. A runaway carriage, Sulai told me. She was thrown out when it overturned.'

'Two hours after she and Jean were married. She was

brought back home directly and the doctor seemed quite sure she would walk again when she recovered from her injuries. Weeks later, when she still lay abed, he could find nothing wrong with her. I brought a specialist here but he said the same thing. Nothing wrong. Marianna could walk if she wished. She did not tell you that?'

'No,' Celina breathed. 'But why, then . . .'

'Does she not make the effort? Who knows? God perhaps, and he alone. I certainly am at a loss to understand it. This may be the beginning of what I have hoped for. This interest of hers now to get out of bed, to belong again. Convince her she is doing the right thing, Celina. She has to believe she can lead a normal life again, be a wife, have children . . .'

Which would stop Jean's philanderings once and for all, Celina mused. If only it was possible to make Marianna believe in herself again. All she needed was the confidence to take that first step. 'Will you help me still?' he said.

'I will do what I can, but not because you ask me, because I am certain you will misconstrue my motives. I'll do it because she is the first person to show me kindness since—since my brother died. I understand the loneliness inside her, for it has been inside me for many years. If I can help her I shall do so gladly.'

'Why I should believe you I don't know, but I do,' Nicholas nodded slowly. 'I'll come up for her at nine. You will dine with us, too—she will expect it.'

'Me?' Celina echoed, 'but . . .'

'In the future, if Marianna comes downstairs, then you will too,' he added, and she knew it would be useless to protest further.

*   *   *

'I think you have made a very foolish gesture.' Jean looked across the table at his wife and his tone bore out his displeasure. He had been in a bad mood when he joined the others in the dining-room, and the sight of Marianna sitting in a chair, wearing the dress she had worn on the night of their elopement, her red hair dressed and glittering with jewels, did nothing to improve his temper. 'A brave but foolish gesture, my dear. I do not wish to see you hurt any more. Haven't you suffered enough? To suffer also the delusion that you might some day walk again . . .'

'Everything is possible,' Nicholas drawled from the head of the table. 'Are you not overjoyed that your wife has joined us? I prefer her company to yours any day.'

'Nicholas,' Marianna reproved, afraid that the enmity which existed between them would rise up again to spoil the evening.

'As I said, a gesture,' Jean replied with a shrug of his shoulders. His eyes rested thoughtfully on the silent figure beside his wife, dressed in a sombre grey gown, her hair pulled back into a mass of tousled curls at the nape of her neck. 'Whose idea was it? Yours, I suppose?'

Celina looked up and met his accusing gaze unflinchingly. In the garden the day before, when he had accosted her and threatened to come to her room if she did not go to his, she had told him she knew about Sulai and the other women he consorted with and would tell Marianna if he did not leave her alone. He had laughed in her face and said she would never do that. He had been right; she could not hurt the girl with such news, especially now when she was feeling in such high spirits. No more could she turn to Nicholas. She had seen him watching from the veranda and known that, had she approached him, he would never have believed she had not encouraged Jean's attentions. What was she to do?

'I am happy to say it was Celina's.' Marianna answered for her and she heaved a sigh of relief that she was not brought into the conversation. Jean was spoiling what had started out to be a pleasant evening.

She had never been in the dining-room before. It was a long, low room, with an enormous fireplace at one end, which took up almost a complete wall. Above it hung the portrait of a strikingly attractive woman with flame-red hair. The first mistress of Paraíso, Elizabeth Benedict, daughter of a Jamaican ship-owner. There was an air of tranquillity about the features, as though she was at peace with herself and the whole world, Celina thought. She knew she had died giving birth to Marianna at the early age of twenty-nine. Nicholas had been fourteen. Her husband had been heartbroken at his loss and could not bring himself to gaze on the small wailing bundle that had cost the life of the woman he loved. As the years passed and she grew into a beautiful child, resembling her mother in looks, he had turned from her even more. Marianna had grown to womanhood hardly realising she had a father. His place had been taken by Nicholas.

Eight years later a new mistress resided at Paraíso, a beautiful Spanish girl Captain John Benedict had brought back with him from one of his long sea-trips. And there the stories she had heard became only rumour. Of conflict between father and son over the new arrival, of nights when Soledad Benedict was reportedly seen stealing into the room of the son, not the husband. Of Marianna's dislike, bordering on hatred, of the woman who treated her like a child. As she looked down the table at Nicholas, disturbingly elegant and handsome in velvet jacket and white ruffled shirt, she remembered something Marianna had blurted out the day

Celina had come to Paraíso. 'It's all right for you to have your amusements, no matter whom you hurt in the process . . .' Had he taken his father's wife, his own stepmother, to his bed? Was he capable of that? Arrogant and selfish, Marianna called him. Did he, like Jean, take his pleasures where and when it suited him?

The face of the dark-haired woman in Kingston rose up to haunt her. His mistress! Perhaps it was true. When she had attempted to find out more about the second Mistress Benedict, her maid had grown agitated and pretended not to hear her questions, and Sulai's arrival had terminated the conversation. All Celina knew was that she had died in an accident somewhere along the cliffs. Why it should suddenly trouble her, she did not know.

She became aware of Nicholas's gaze, his eyes gleaming with amusement as he caught the intensity of her scrutiny. She had been so lost in thought that she had been staring at him for several minutes. Colour flooding into her cheeks, she resumed her meal.

She had eaten well since arriving at Paraíso. Too well, she thought, looking down at the slices of roast duckling on her plate. She was putting on pounds. Her new dresses would not fit her in a month's time if she continued at this rate.

'I am sailing to Kingston next week,' Nicholas said some time later. 'Is there anything you want me to pick up for you, Marianna?'

'Perfume and ribbons and some new shoes. I can hardly get my wretched swollen feet into the ones I have. And I would dearly love some dress material. I watched Celina being fitted by Madame Irene and I was so envious . . . I didn't realise how much at the time. I should have ordered something. You could pick up Celina's dresses if you like. They will be ready by Thursday.'

'Ah, yes, Celina's new wardrobe,' Nicholas murmured, and she looked at him instantly. Had he changed his mind? Was she not to have it after all? She had been most careful to choose the plainest of materials and designs. It would not do for her, a companion, to be seen dressed as elegantly as Marianna. 'I spoke with Madame before she left, to approve Celina's choice of garments, naturally.'

Naturally, Celina thought, and then his next words quite took her breath away.

'They were unsuitable, all of them. Dull colours, plain designs. I am surprised you did not advise her, Marianna. Do you want her to look like an old maid? I have ordered more suitable attire.'

No, that is what I want, Celina almost cried out, so that you do not accuse me of enticing men's eyes to me ever again. *He* had chosen her wardrobe! She could hardly believe her ears.

'Well, well,' Jean said softly. 'Are we about to paint the lily?'

'Celina has a position to uphold here,' Nicholas retorted sharply. 'When Marianna begins to go out and about again she will want to go visiting, maybe even come on a trip to Kingston with me. Celina will need suitable clothes for such occasions. I am merely thinking ahead.'

'As always,' Jean chuckled, drinking the wine in his glass and motioning Xavier to refill it. The sly minx—so she was, after all, Nicholas's exclusive property. No wonder she had refused his invitations! She was afraid of losing what she already had . . . and the prospect of more to come. He raised his glass in Celina's direction. 'To the new mistress—of Paraíso.'

'Jean, don't talk in riddles,' Marianna said, her pretty face becoming concerned as she realised he had been drinking heavily for some time. He held it well, but when it seized hold of him she had discovered a different side to the man she had fallen helplessly in love with and braved her brother's wrath to marry. For what? She had never shared his bed, and he had grown tired of waiting. What he could not have from her, he took from others. She was not as blind as everyone thought and she knew his eyes were straying now in the direction of Celina. At all costs, she must save her from him. If only she had the courage to speak to Nicholas, break down the barriers between them that she herself had erected in her anger and grief—and shame. 'I am mistress here and always will be, although I must admit Celina has had more experience of running a house than I have. If necessary, I shall learn from her. It is not too late for me to learn anything, Jean.'

Conscious of Nicholas's eyes on him, Jean blew her a kiss across the table.

'My dear, I apologise for my boorish manners. Your brother is working me damnably hard, and I am tired. If only I could spend more time with you . . .'

'That can easily be arranged. Why don't you take Marianna out in the carriage tomorrow,' Nicholas suggested with a slight smile. 'I will take Celina on a tour of the plantation. I don't think she has been further than the gardens, has she, Marianna?'

'No, indeed she has not. What a wonderful idea. But only if you promise to be nice to her.'

'I shall be on my best behaviour, I promise,' Nicholas vowed. 'Do you ride, Celina?'

'Why—yes, but not for several years . . . I don't think . . .'

'Of course you are going,' Marianna interrupted. 'I have monopolised you for three whole weeks.'

'It is why she is here,' Jean reminded her, but she ignored the comment. With Nicholas, Celina would be safe and it would give her a chance to talk to Jean. A talk long overdue. How she had grown up in these past weeks, she thought, and it was all due to Celina.

'Very well. If I must.' Ride, with him! Why was he being so nice to her all of a sudden—it was highly suspicious? Those blue eyes danced with wicked lights, and she quickly looked away.

Celina left Marianna in high spirits, awaiting Jean's arrival to take her out in the carriage. Her first drive since the night of her accident. She was not to know how the smile was wiped from the face of the other girl the moment the door had closed behind her.

Nicholas was waiting for her in the entrance hall. As he heard the swish of her skirts, he turned and appraised her appearance. Sulai had been clever enough to guess Celina's measurements, enabling Madame Irene to bring several more garments with her, including several blouses and the riding-skirt Celina now wore. Neat brown leather boots showed beneath the hem and she had chosen a pale-coloured blouse to offset the sombre colour of the skirt. Her hair was tied back with a matching ribbon and she carried a pair of brown leather gloves. A creature of elegance and beauty, Nicholas mused, nodding his head as if she met with his approval.

Two horses were saddled and waiting for them, a large black stallion, and a white-stockinged bay which he indicated was for her. She mounted awkwardly, conscious of how easily he had swung his large frame into the saddle. She had never been a good rider, as she had preferred to walk along the cliffs and watch the seagulls. Her brother had been the horseman.

He went at a leisurely pace which she did not find difficult to keep up with, and after a short while she found herself beginning to relax and enjoy the unexpected outing. She hoped Jean and Marianna would find pleasure in theirs, too. The sun was warm on her face and on her neck where the open collar fluttered wide in a light breeze. They passed rows of cabins where the slaves lived and, further on, more cabins set aside from the others. She saw children playing and women washing clothes. The lilt of an accent made her glance at Nicholas sharply.

'You are not the only Scottish exile here. I've a dozen men, some with wives,' he said, as if he had been waiting for the question.

'Indentured, like me?'

'Most of them. On paper only. As far as I am concerned, they are free.'

But not me, she almost said, but, realising he was expecting such a remark, she wisely made no comment. They looked well cared for, she thought, as they continued on. No signs of ill-treatment on any of the faces curiously looking her way.

They would know about her, of course. There were few secrets at Paraíso. Those that existed were well kept. Like the mystery surrounding the death of the Spanish wife of John Benedict and Nicholas's closeness to the 'Fox', the privateer whose intervention at sea had prevented their ship from being attacked by the French man o'war. Had they been taken, she might be free now, in Martinique perhaps, not riding beside Nicholas beneath tall, shady trees, with the sweet smell of exotic wild orchids all around her. They bloomed in abundance in the hot sun.

She could feel her cheeks beginning to glow. Against her will she was accepting Paraíso, with the many advantages which came from being there, as her home. Beneath lowered lashes, she glanced at the sunburnt profile beside her. His gaze was intent on the fields ahead where the last of the cutting was taking place and, unlike the night before, he was unaware of her scrutiny. What was the reason for this sudden invitation? She hoped it was in order to give Marianna a chance to be alone with her husband and perhaps to repair some of the damage her long confinement in bed had brought about. She did not want to believe that there was an ulterior motive lurking somewhere in his mind. No, why should there be? He could demand her company at any time without a specific reason.

They rode alongside fields where the huge tobacco leaves had been cut and were lying in the sun. Tomorrow, he told her, they would be gathered, as many already had been, and taken to the sheds ahead of them.

Nicholas hooked a booted foot over the pommel of his saddle and reached for a cheroot from his shirt-pocket. This year's harvest would be one of the best in the history of Paraíso. With the money from the tobacco sale he intended to begin a very special undertaking, if the 'Fox' gave him permission. He would search the old rascal out and put the idea to him, when next in Kingston.

'Would you like to see what goes on next?' he asked. 'The next step in the process, or perhaps the whole thing bores you?'

She had not spoken a word to him in the past hour. No

more had he to her, he realised. At times he had been unaware of her presence.

'Am I not in the way?' Celina asked, following suit as he reined in his horse.

'Had I thought so, I would not have brought you. I wanted to leave Marianna and Jean alone for a while; surely you are astute enough to have guessed that.'

'It was in my mind.' Inwardly she gave a sigh of relief. Her fears were groundless. She brushed a damp tendril of hair from her forehead and he smiled at the movement.

'You'll soon grow used to the heat. Do you like it here, Celina? At Paraíso?'

'Yes.' He looked at her sharply, taken aback by the swiftness of her answer. 'I have tried not to like it,' she added, so that he did not consider it a victory. 'I did not want to like Marianna, but who could not like her? And it has been so long since I have been with my own . . . with another woman.'

'With your own kind, you wanted to say,' Nicholas chided. 'I acknowledge life has changed drastically for you over the past two years, but you have survived it well. Reluctantly, too, I must concede Mistress Celina MacNeill is of good stock, whatever she has become since leaving Scotland.'

'Would you insult a lady as you do me?' she challenged. 'You are laughing at me. I hate you!'

'You rouse the devil in me, Celina. This docile mood of yours won't last. Let's ride on. I told Sulai to prepare a cold lunch back at the house for us at noon.'

He was quite insufferable! One moment he all but admitted he had been wrong and in the next breath he was tossing another of his odious insults at her. One day she would find a way to wipe that smile from his face!

Mule-driven carts, weighed down with tobacco leaves, were heading towards large wooden sheds several hundreds of yards away. Here, Celina found, as she wandered around them with her companion, there were smouldering fires which regulated the heat to around 70 and 80 degrees. The leaves were hung over sticks and left until they were ready to be covered with matting and allowed to 'sweat' for six to eight weeks, being turned every day to ensure equal curing. It was a long and complicated process, she thought, as she emerged into the sunlight again, her cheeks now a bright red from the fires. Even Nicholas's face was wet with perspiration, and he paused to take a dipper of water from the water-boy who approached him, filled it, and handed it to her. She drank gratefully. Her throat felt parched. He followed suit and then ran a hand through his thick blond hair as he looked up at the sun.

'Almost mid-day. We should be starting back.'

Xavier came threading his way through the wagons waiting to be unloaded as they walked back towards their horses. Negroes and whites worked side by side on Paraíso, Celina had discovered. She had heard the heart-warming sound of Scots voices in the sheds and longed to ask what names they went by, but dared not lest Nicholas misconstrue her motives. There were ebony-skinned men among the workers who spoke in a dialect only they seemed to comprehend, and lighter-skinned mulattos like Sulai, who spoke Spanish. Very few used the English tongue, as the Scotsmen conversed in Gaelic.

'Captain, we have more sick men. Another three. Will you come and look at them?'

Celina was no longer surprised wherever Xavier turned up. In the house he was always at Nicholas's side, but she had discovered that Sulai went to him for her instructions, as did the rest of the servants. Only the other day she had seen him breaking in a wild horse, one of a dozen Nicholas had purchased in Kingston and which had just arrived overland at Paraíso. It seemed that he was also someone of importance out in the plantation. Surely this was Jean's job, not his, and then she remembered that the latter was with Marianna. How lucky Nicholas was to have someone on hand to slip into the position of trust. If she had not known otherwise, Celina would never have taken him for a slave. He was well-mannered and exceedingly well educated, being able to read and write, which none of the other house servants could do, not even Sulai.

'Damnation!' Nicholas said, and a flicker of annoyance crossed his features. 'More of them? What does the doctor have to say, or is he still ignorant of the cause? Never mind, I'll speak to him myself. Let's take a look at them. Wait in the cool of those trees yonder, Celina, as I may be some while.'

She found a shaded place, spread her skirts and sat down. The plantation stretched for miles, she thought, straining her eyes to try to see where the fields ended, but they seemed to go on and on endlessly. No wonder such a large work-force was needed to care for it. It was well run by a capable and, when necessary, ruthless man. There was comfort and to a certain extent freedom. It was not a bad thing to be part of such an establishment, she thought, better than working in someone's kitchen, washing clothes and dishes until her hands were raw. Better than belonging to a man like Lester. She shuddered despite the warmth of the day. Nicholas Benedict was the shadow on her sun, but Marianna made up for that, and Sulai and all the other

friends she had made in the house is three short weeks.
They had accepted her presence among them without
question. She was pretty sure that there were many
speculative rumours, but so far none had reached her
ears. They could not malign her any more than the
master of Paraíso himself did.

Huge mountains towered in the distance, along their
slopes a mass of dark green vegetation. The island itself
was over one hundred miles in length and some fifty
miles wide, with Kingston as its main port, since old Port
Royal had been destroyed in a terrible earthquake in
1692. Once the latter had been the most flourishing
English city in the New World. Sulai knew everything
about Kingston, having lived there most of her life, and
Celina had learned much from her about Jamaica. She
knew the Indian name meant 'Well wooded and
watered', and that was certainly true. She had seen at
least four separate streams cutting through the land on
her morning ride, and another behind the drying-sheds.
And everywhere there were trees. The timber was used
for building on Paraíso. When a tree was felled, a young
sapling was replanted to take its place and keep the
numbers constant.

Behind the house she had found groves of lime trees
bordering fields of vegetables. Paraíso was self-sufficient
in every way. As self-sufficient as the man who owned it!

A startled oath off to one side of her brought her out
of her dreamy state. A man stood a few feet away,
staring at her from beneath bushy brows. He was heavily
bearded, his skin tanned deeply. As were most of the
workers she had seen, he was dressed in a homespun
shirt and well-worn trousers. There was something
familiar about the face! No, it was not possible! She
could know no one from home, much as she longed for a

familiar countenance. And yet?

'Celina? Is it you? Dear God, is it really you?'

The face she did not recognise, not with the heavy beard hiding most of it and a thatch of unruly hair obscuring his eyes to give him an appearance that was somewhat ferocious, but she knew the voice. She had thought never to hear it again. He was dead! They had told her he had died after they dragged him from beside her and his struggles had brought the butt of a musket down across his head. His blood had soaked her skirt as they hauled him away like a carcass of meat.

'David,' she whispered in disbelief. 'You are alive!'

She was caught up in a hug that squeezed the breath from her body. He was never this strong, she thought, as she flung her arms about his neck and smothered the bearded face with kisses.

'Davie, how are you here? Do you belong to him too? This is a miracle. I can't believe it! Tell me I'm not dreaming? Hold me. Hold me and tell me this is real?'

'Let me look at you.' David MacNeill put his sister at arm's length and examined her face for a long moment. 'I prayed for us to be together again, but not like this. Not here, as work horses, although you seem to have fared better than most and I thank God for that. You promised me you would not sign the papers.' He meant the papers of indentureship which very few Highlanders signed willingly.

'I did not,' Celina protested softly. 'My signature was forged. It happened all the time when they needed to fill a prison ship.'

'Dear heaven! You went through that, too.' All those weeks at sea!

She touched his cheek, his mouth, tracing the outlines that were so dear to her, and there were tears in her eyes.

'You have grown . . . and you look like a wild man with that beard. Oh, Davie, I don't care what happens to me now I have found you.'

'What do you mean?' His eyes fastened on her clothes and narrowed sharply with suspicion. 'Did he buy you too? How long have you been here?'

'Only three weeks. I am well treated. Companion to his sister, Marianna.'

'The cripple. I've heard about her, seen her once or twice. Pretty little thing. A pity about that womanising husband of hers. No female on the place is safe with him around. You have not been mistreated? If you have . . .'

'No, oh no,' she cried. 'I have my own rooms and a servant and new clothes.'

'You have accepted it, then. A life of servitude?' her brother asked, and her eyes grew dark with reproach.

'I have not! Nor shall I. One day I shall be free and so will you. Together we shall make a life for ourselves, and we shall never be parted again. Hold me, Davie. I am still afraid you will disappear in a puff of smoke!'

'Never! You are right, we shall never be parted again. If anyone tries, I'll kill them,' he said in a fierce whisper, gathering her against him again, pressing his lips against the silkiness of her hair. How good she smelled, reminding him of the French perfumes she had always worn at home.

'Believe me, my friend, she is not worth dying for,' a voice heavy with sarcasm declared behind her.

Celina cried out as a hand fastened over her wrist, jerking her from her brother's grasp. She was flung roughly backwards into Xavier's arms, which folded around her and held her immobile. The expression on Nicholas's face was murderous as he turned to face

David. A well-delivered blow on the jaw sent him crashing to the ground.

'Don't ever touch her again, ' David threatened as, fists bunched, he towered over his employer. 'She's quality, Captain. Do you understand what that means? '

'So she keeps telling me. Know her, do you? Companion in the heather, was she?' Nicholas came to his feet again with the litheness of a panther, side-stepped the swing aimed at his head and sent David staggering back into the waiting arms of two negroes who had come up behind him.

'Davie, don't,' Celina pleaded, as her brother began to struggle furiously, cursing the men who held him, and his employer, in the most descriptive language. He, too, had changed since they were last together, she realised sadly. 'Please, don't make things hard for yourself because of me.' Appealingly she looked at Nicholas. 'He meant no harm.' His jaw was grazed, and his shirt covered in dust. 'He meant only to protect me.'

'Protection is not something you need from anyone,' came the curt retort as he touched his bruised face. 'Good God, I leave you alone for ten minutes and come back to find you in the arms of one of my field-hands. You set your sights too low, Celina. I could give you what you want and you'd be well rewarded for your trouble.'

David gave a strangled cry and tried to launch himself at the other man, incensed by the insult which brought embarrassed colour into his sister's cheeks. Well cared for, she said, yet this man looked at her as if . . . He was forced to his knees by the men holding him, his arms twisted painfully behind his back until he became still.

'Don't hurt him,' Celina whispered. The last time she had seen him he had been on his knees, blood pouring from his head. She felt sick and faint with the memory. 'You don't understand, Captain Benedict, please let me speak . . .'

'Don't beg from him, for God's sake,' her brother cried hoarsely. 'He'd not be standing there so smug if my hands were free. If I had a sword . . .'

'You would defend her honour?' Nicholas mocked. 'I've told you she isn't worth it.'

'To me, she is. Are you not man enough to fight to keep what you have bought, Captain?'

'If you were not so useful to me, I would take you up on your offer . . .'

'You can find another doctor to tend your men! I'll not lay another finger on them to help you.'

Doctor! Her brother was the doctor she had heard spoken of, who looked after the sick workers.

'No, Davie! You were meant to heal, not kill. Don't start again.'

'Davie,' Nicholas drawled. 'So this is the lover who haunts your dreams. Let her go, Xavier. Take this man away and lock him up somewhere secure. Tomorrow at seven in the morning I want him brought to the house. He shall have his chance.'

'I'll kill you!' David spat the words at him, eyes blazing as he was dragged away. Celina crumpled to the ground, near to fainting, as she was released. This could not happen, she must tell the truth.

'Up with you.' Nicholas hauled her to her feet and pushed her roughly towards the horses. 'It's too late to feel sorry for what you have done.'

'You cannot fight him, you can't.' She was aghast at the prospect. 'He's not a swordsman. He used one in the uprising, but his heart was not in it. You'll kill him. I won't let you.'

'What would you do to save his life, Celina?' Nicholas asked, and her eyes widened with sudden resolve.

'Anything. I love him enough to do anything. ' It was the truth.

His expression was icy as he helped her to mount. The rage welling inside him as he looked at her was terrible in its fury. Only once before had he ever felt this way towards a woman—and she was dead!

'We shall see,' was the only answer which came back to her. It frightened her more than if he had demanded her presence in his bed that night. She had until seven in the morning. What could she do in that time? Looking into Nicholas's cold eyes, she knew it would not be too long before he told her .

CHAPTER
FIVE

THE RETURN to the house was even worse than Celina anticipated. As they neared it, Jean rode past them at a gallop, neither acknowledging them nor moving his mount aside to give them passage, and both had to wheel their horses aside to avoid a collision. What had happened to put him in such a foul temper, she wondered, watching Nicholas's face darken with anger? He had not spoken a word to her on the way back, nor had he looked even once in her direction. She felt like a leper! How dare he treat her so callously? Had he no heart? Yet even his mood could not take away the happiness she had rediscovered. David, her brother, was alive and she would do anything necessary to ensure his safety, even if it meant becoming the kind of woman Nicholas Benedict thought her to be. No sacrifice was too great, not for her brother. Had he not saved her life time and time again as they hid in the mountains from the soldiers, had he not stolen food so that she should not go hungry, and sat and watched while his own stomach protested?

Such a gentle person he had once been. The man who had leapt to her defence with clenched fists had not surprised her, but the fury in his eyes, the threat in his voice, they had! His life had been dedicated to healing, and the saving of lives. He was not and never had been a fighter. Prison and the aftermath had changed him, as it had her. He was a man now well able to take care of himself, given the chance, and Nicholas had granted him that.

Was it his intention to kill David? Why should it trouble him that he had found her in the arms of another man?

Leaping from his horse, Nicholas strode ahead of her into the house and upstairs to his sister's room. Celina hovered outside, not wanting to intrude, and heard the sound of angry voices. Marianna was obviously in distress, and, unable to bear the sobbing, Celina went in. Nicholas wheeled on her, eyes like blazing sapphires focusing on her.

'Leave us,' he thundered.

Celina took one look at the tearful figure in bed, and ignored him. She heard an oath as she gathered Marianna in her arms and rocked her as though she were a small child.

'Hush, it cannot be as bad as all that. Tell me. Tell me what is wrong,' she soothed gently, and Marianna raised a red, tearful face to her and began to weep again.

'He did not want to be seen with me. I am a cripple. He hates me! Oh, Celina, what have I done? Is no one to love me now?'

'Silly goose, I love you. Your brother loves you. Stop this nonsense now!' Celina ordered in a sharper tone. 'He is a fool if he does not appreciate what he has, so let him go to the devil. Must you suffer for his stupidity? Sit up! Look at these eyes? This morning they were shining. How wretched you look. I'll ring for your maid, and in a few minutes I'll have you smiling again.'

'He doesn't want me,' Marianna whispered against her shoulder. 'It has all been for nothing, as I knew it would.'

'Nonsense. What you have achieved has been for yourself as well as for Jean. If you think I am going to let you sit in bed for the rest of your days because of his unreasonable attitude, you are wrong. Tonight I shall find the prettiest dress in your closet and you will go down to dinner. Are the Benedicts not made of tough fibre? Do they disintegrate at the slightest hurdle?'

She had forgotten the presence of Nicholas behind her until she turned away to pull the bell-rope and saw him watching her. He was standing quite still, an expression she had never seen before on his face. A mixture of contempt and incredulity! Let him think what he pleased, she was too occupied with Marianna to care, and her own problems had disappeared, at least for the moment, into the background. When the maid came, Celina ordered warm water and clean towels to be brought and a light lunch. When she looked for Nicholas again, he had gone.

Marianna refused to go downstairs that evening, and nothing Celina said could persuade her otherwise. They dined together in her bedroom, but Celina ate as little as her companion. As the hours wore on she began to remember that she and Nicholas were drawing closer to a terrible confrontation—perhaps the last between them. One of them would surely lose, and it would not be he! He already considered her no better than a common whore. Anything she did would be misinterpreted.

Celina stayed with her until almost midnight. She tried to draw her out on what had happened, but the girl had refused to say anything other than that Jean had refused to be seen with her. Marianna had said nothing of the accusations and recriminations she had heaped on his head for the last twelve months she had spent in bed, all due to him. He had laughed at her outrage, offered to comfort her if she was so desperate for his company, and she had screamed at him to leave her. She had wanted not his sympathy, but his love. A love she now knew had never existed for him, only for her, and now, this day, that was dead! She had told him so with such scorn that she had seen him look unsure of himself for the first time ever. He had slapped her hard and warned her against confiding in her brother, or anyone who might aid her against him. She knew he meant Celina. His anger had terrified her. How she wished she had the use of her legs! She would get out of bed, walk unaided and tell him to leave Paraíso for ever because she no longer needed him. She did not need him now, did not want him, but while she lay abed, helpless and at his mercy, she knew she would have to guard her tongue. He was a dangerous man, devious and cruel. She was only now discovering how cruel. Her arms and wrists still ached from the way he had grabbed her and thrown her back on to the pillows, threatening her with all kinds of dire consequences if she dared open her mouth to anyone. The job of overseer suited him for the moment, he told her, a smile on the sallow features, and she was not to spoil it for him. When he chose to go, he would, and she could not stop him. Go! Go now, she had begged, but he had laughed again and left her to her tears and her self-reproach and her secrets.

Wearily, Celina entered her own room when, eventually, Marianna had fallen into an exhausted sleep. She had understood only half of what the bedridden girl had said in her agitation. There was much she had unburdened and much she had kept to herself. Paraíso was fast becoming a house full of secrets, Celina thought, as she crossed to the windows and opened them.

Alone, she turned her thoughts to her own problems. Tomorrow David would cross swords with Nicholas Benedict. Instinctively she knew the latter was master of his weapon, whereas her brother was not and would pay dearly for it unless she did something. But what?

She became aware of the aroma of smoke in the room. Turning slowly, she knew whom she would see, even before the glow of a cheroot indicated the presence of Nicholas in a chair beside the sofa.

'Is my sister asleep now?'

'Yes.' What did he want of her? How long had he been sitting alone in the darkness waiting for her? She felt physically drained of strength and knew she could fight him no longer. Whatever price he demanded for David's life, she would pay it. He could think no less of her than he already did.

'We Benedicts are not accustomed to airing our differences before outsiders,' he said coldly. 'Marianna was overwrought.'

'Do you ever air your differences, Captain, or do you keep them locked away inside you?' she challenged. Did he understand so little of his sister? Could he not see she was deeply troubled? 'Marianna is very unhappy. I don't know why, only that it has little to do with her accident. With her husband, perhaps, yet even then I sense there must be more to have brought about such a state. This morning she was so happy and determined to continue with the progress she has made this past week. Something terrible lies between them, something neither you nor I can make her tell us. I find that sad. I am only her companion, but you are her brother, yet she has not confided in you.'

'She will, in time.' Nicholas rose to his feet, crushing out the half-smoked cheroot in an ashtray on the table beside him. *She* was presuming to tell *him* he did not understand his own sister! He did not know how long he had been waiting for her. He had not eaten downstairs, but had shut himself in his room after an unpleasant encounter with Jean, which had almost come to blows. And then, without reason, he had come to her room and sat in the darkness and waited for her.

Why had he come? To remonstrate further with her for her scandalous behaviour, he told himself as he sat in the silence and pondered his actions. Why should he bother? Why did he not just sell her and be rid of her tantalising presence once and for all. He could always find another companion for his sister, once with less colourful a reputation. He could not sell Celina. He had wanted her for himself from the first moment he saw her in Antigua. Marianna had been an excuse, but only now did he admit it to himself. He had never done anything like this before. He was a man who always had a sound reason for all his actions. To buy a woman because her sad eyes had touched his misogynist's heart! It angered him beyond reason, as the sight of her held in the arms of another man had done. She had flinched from his, been contemptuous of his kisses, yet she welcomed those of a field-hand.

The man Davie was known to her. Neither had denied it. In the darkness he had dwelt on the months they had spent together in the heather, the closeness of their relationship, and his temper had not improved. If she took up with anyone, Nicholas would be the man! The sooner she accepted that, the better.

He moved across the room towards her and took her in his arms. Celina felt faint with horror, yet she made no

move to release herself from his embrace. His lips
caressed her cheek, her throat, the smooth hollow above
her breasts and then lifted to seek her mouth in the
darkness. His kisses had a wildness about them that sent
a shiver of fear through her.

'Is there a difference between his arms and mine?'
Nicholas asked harshly. 'His kisses and mine? Which do
you prefer?'

'You don't understand,' Celina whispered, hating
herself for the way her body was so swiftly aroused by
the touch of his hands. 'Let me speak, please.'

'I want no lies! If you will warm anyone's bed, it will be
mine.'

'Which is why you bought me,' she cried, throwing
back her head to stare into the face above her. 'Do you
think I didn't see how you looked at me that day? How
many other poor wretches have you bought and seduced
under one pretext or another? Are pickings so lean on
the Caribbean these days?' She flung the words at him
that Lester had used, and heard a sharp exclamation.
She no more knew what it meant now than she had then,
but the meaning was not lost on Nicholas, for his fingers
tightened painfully over her shoulders.

'You would do well not to throw that in my face,
Mistress, ignorant as you are of its meaning.'

'What will you do? Beat me? Sell me? I have been
beaten before, my character maligned until my name is a
dirty word. Get rid of me, then. I care not what you do
with me.'

'And your lover? What of him? You would like me to
sell the pair of you, perhaps, so that you could be
together. No, that will not happen.' Nicholas dragged
her up against him, pressing kisses on her mouth between his words until she sagged spent and breathless in

his arms. 'Tomorrow you will watch me kill him. A lesson to others who think you are available.'

'No!' Celina screamed the word at him, beat her clenched fists against his chest. 'You vile monster. You will not! I shall not let it happen. Not now. We have only just found each other again.' She began to sob in helpless terror. He was unapproachable; his mind closed to her pleas! Dear God, what possessed him? Of course she was his property. No other man must touch what belonged to Nicholas Benedict! 'I shall do anything— anything, do you hear? Just let him live. Sell me, but let him live. Whip me, starve me . . .' A sob caught in her throat. She became still and suddenly quiet and for a long moment she did not speak. Then, in a voice she did not recognise as her own, she said, 'I will be the wanton you believe me to be if you will let my brother live.'

'Brother!' Nicholas's incredulous tone sounded a thousand miles away as her knees buckled and only his arms prevented her from falling to the floor. She felt herself lifted and carried a short distance and, as her senses slowly returned, found he had laid her on the sofa and placed a cushion behind her head. A glass was held against her lips. 'Drink it,' he ordered when she uttered a feeble protest, and she swallowed a mouthful of the red wine. The room continued to revolve around her for another few minutes. The terrible decision to commit herself to the final humiliating act she had avoided for so long had brought her to breaking-point. She had offered herself to him! Confirmation indeed of everything he had believed about her!

The hand that Nicholas clasped was like ice. He had to see her face and know if this was yet another ruse to sway him from his chosen path. She did not move as he left her to light the oil lamp. He brought it to the table beside the

sofa and put it down so that the light was full on her face.
Her skin looked like wax. The wide violet eyes had the
look of a little lost child.

'If this is another lie . . .'

'Do you still wish to know about Celina MacNeill?
Then I shall tell you, but I hate you for making me do so.
The secrets you tear from me were not meant for your
ears, for anyone's. They belong to me. You tell me to
forget the past, but you shall hear them.'

She told him everything, sparing herself no pain,
letting not one little detail escape description. Let him
know how it was. The horror of war for the innocent, the
butchery for brave men who had fought valiantly for
their Prince. He would not understand—how could
he?—but he would know. She told him first of her home,
Craig Tor, and her family. Father, mother, David and
sister. Of the fateful day Charles Stuart had raised his
standard at Glenfinnan, and all the men of the glen able
to hold a weapon had gone to join him, leaving behind
only women and children and those too old to fight.

She told him of those long months when she and her
family had waited for news of the Prince's advance into
England, dreading that someone would return with
news of the death of father of brother. The retreat and
the infamous Battle of Culloden, when Highlanders had
been cut down in their hundreds by grapeshot and
cannon-fire, and how she had watched it, alongside
many people from Inverness, on a hill overlooking the
moor that would never be forgotten in the memories of
any Highlander. Her voice broke with the tumult of
emotion which claimed her, as she began the graphic
description of her descent to the battleground as clans
broke and fled under the withering English fire and the
watchers knew the battle was lost.

'You went looking for your father and brother?' It was the first time Nicholas had spoken. He had drawn up a chair beside her and sat with his arms folded over his chest in an attitude that told her he was prepared to disbelieve every word she said. 'Amid that carnage?'

'I had to find them,' she replied simply. When she closed her eyes, how swiftly that scene came back to her. The dead and dying lying in the heather. The acrid smell of cannon-smoke hanging in the air, the odour of blood and death! 'It was two hours before I found Father. A sabre had cut him almost in two.' How calmly she now related what, at the time, had made her turn away and vomit into the grass. She had almost given up then as her courage deserted her. Then the calls of the wounded as they pleaded for water, calling out the names of their loved ones as they lay abandoned, defeated, awaiting the coming of the English in the morning who were, unbeknownst then, to bayonet those still left alive, to strip them of clothes and valuables and bury them in mass graves like nameless paupers, made her weak legs continue.

David had been lying a few yards away, unconscious from a head wound. She had fetched water from a nearby burn and bathed it. At last he had recovered consciousness, but for a week, as she guided him towards home, he had not known her. He had cursed her ministerings, begged her to leave him to die, and cursed her again when she forced him on. When he recovered his faculties, it was like a miracle, and together they had slowly made their way to Craig Tor.

Nothing remained but stones and blackened crofts. The soldiers had been there two days earlier, a survivor told them. Their mother and sister, murdered after heaven only knew what abuses they had been forced to suffer by their appearances, had been left in the court-yard amid slain servant-women and retainers. She and David had dug two graves away from the others. She had wept and collapsed and known nothing more for days.

This time it was David who carried her from hiding-place to hiding-place, stole food to keep her alive, cradled her in his arms when the nightmares began from which she awoke screaming in terror. They endured six months of animal existence until they were skin and bone, the clothes on their backs little more than rags. There was nothing left to steal in the Highlands; the soldiers saw to that as they relentlessly drove the elusive rebels before them, cornered them, slew or arrested them and sent them to stinking English gaols to languish in filth.

Somehow she and David managed to stay together after their capture. They had no money, nothing of value to sell after she had parted with her diamond earrings and the bracelet he had given her for her eighteenth birthday. These kept them in warm surroundings, with food in their mouths, if it could be called that, for three whole months. After that they were transported back to a common gaol, with hundreds in the same plight.

'They came one day and asked us to sign papers,' she whispered. 'We would become indentured servants, but in time would be free. We had heard rumours of trans-portations. You cannot feel as we did. You cannot know what it is like to tell a Highlander he must leave his beloved land, never see it again. David would not sign. No more would I, but they came again and again. He lost his temper when they tried to force him, struck one of the officers . . . They dragged him away, blood on his head and face. Next day they told me he had died. A week later I was put aboard the prison ship for Antigua.

Someone had signed my name on the indenture papers. I would rather have died in prison than sign.'

'Then, perhaps. What about now?' Nicholas leaned towards her.

'Now?' She shrugged her still thin shoulders. 'Nothing seems to matter any more, except that I have found Davie again.'

His mind dazed by the vivid account of her suffering, the hardships she had endured before he met her, Nicholas rose and turned towards the door. Her eyes followed him uncomprehendingly. Was he leaving? Nothing had been settled.

'What are you going to do tomorrow?' she whispered, starting up. 'I am begging for his life, Captain Benedict. I have never begged from anyone before. Neither the prison gaolers who offered me a warm bed and food if I would sleep with them, nor the first officer aboard the ship. My pride was the only thing left to sustain me when I thought David was dead. But somehow, now, that doesn't matter any more. Please don't hurt him. Please!'

Across the room, Nicholas's gaze lingered on the pale face and trembling lips. She was his for the taking! But he knew that to take advantage of her would be the most contemptible act he had ever committed. Memories had drained her of strength, of resistance. For a moment he was tempted to send for the brother to comfort her, but that would have presaged capitulation on his part, and he did not like to announce his intentions ahead of time. His jaw still ached from the blow David had dealt him. The morning would be soon enough to make his peace with them both.

'I will send your maid to you. Go to bed and rest,' he ordered.

Celina sank back on the sofa as the door closed behind him. She had told him everything about herself in a desperate attempt to arouse pity in him, and she had failed. It was the most crushing blow life had ever dealt her, and she did not know what to do next, for she had nothing left to fight with. She had offered herself to him, yet she went to bed alone! He would come back again later, she told herself. Had he not categorically stated that she would belong to him and to no one else? Her lips were bruised from his kisses. Kisses that had both thrilled and frightened her. How long could she endure them without giving herself away?

He had sat like a statue while she spoke, his features impassive. Not once did he show any sign of surprise or concern and had asked only one question of her throughout. How could anyone be so unfeeling? Without wanting to, she slept.

She awoke to the sound of a quarrel outside the window, which overlooked the paddock area and the stables where Nicholas maintained a fine string of pure-bred horses, many of Arab strain. Her mind still fogged with sleep, she lay listening to the heated encounter until memory suddenly came flooding back and, with it, the realisation it was past seven.

Snatching up a robe, she thrust her feet into slippers and ran to the window. Below, Nicholas and David faced each other. Both held swords! Xavier and several coloured hands stood off to one side. Arms folded, Jean was leaning against a fence, a smile on his face as he watched the two combatants. As if he would enjoy a fight in which one of them would surely be killed, she thought in disgust. David was a stranger to him, so it had to be Nicholas he was hoping to see despatched. Startled servants stepped aside, and she ran through the corridors, down the staircase, brushing past Sulai, without even seeing her, and out into the crisp morning air by a side door which took her direct to where the encounter was taking place. She had to stop it, but how?

'I have offered you an apology, MacNeill. There is no need for us to cross swords.' She came to an abrupt halt a few yards away as Nicholas's voice came clearly to her. She could not believe she had heard aright. He was prepared to tender an apology! Then why were they holding swords? Why did her brother look so fierce? 'If you force this on me, I shall kill you, and there is no reason.'

'I have reason enough to kill you,' David snapped. 'To free my sister from bondage.'

'Taking my life will not do that. Only my signature of her papers or a pardon from the Governor.'

'Damn you,' David ejaculated fiercely and lunged at him. Nicholas side-stepped with the ease of an accomplished swordsman, his own weapon coming up to defend himself.

'No,' Celina cried, running towards them. 'Stop it!' Xavier caught and held her fast, dragging her back from danger. 'Let me go. They must not fight!'

'There is nothing you can do, Mistress Celina. It is your brother's choice, not the captain's.'

She thrust her hands over her ears to shut out the sound of the clashing blades. David fought well, but wildly, she saw, quickly exhausting his strength, whereas Nicholas's movements were controlled and purposeful. He was playing with her brother as he had with her, knowing at all times he had the upper hand. Had her brother been returned to her safe and well only to be taken from her after a few hours?

Nicholas gave a grunt of pain, and she caught her

breath as she saw blood seeping through the sleeve of his shirt. He stepped back, lowering his sword.

'First blood to you, and well deserved, as is the apology I now offer, whether you wish to accept it or not, MacNeill. I'll not fight further with you. Besides, I need the services of a good doctor. My men are on the road to recovery and it is all due to you. I have a proposition I think might interest you, if you will put aside your weapon and listen.'

'What trickery is this?' David stared at him, taken aback. His opponent's sword was lowered, leaving his body unguarded. One thrust and he would be dead. So would he, David knew, and where would that leave Celina then? Xavier had been quite specific about what would happen to him if Nicholas Benedict died at his hands.

Nicholas looked across to Celina. He had hoped to spare her further pain by averting the fight, but her brother was as stubborn as she was. What a pair they were!

She looked as pale and drawn as when he had left her, and he guessed she had slept very little. Little fool! Why had she come down to watch?

'Your sister will not lie to you,' he said. 'Ask her.'

'Do I trust him, Celina?' David, too, stared at the slim figure, clutching together a silk pink robe as Xavier released her. He knew he stood no chance against Nicholas in a prolonged bout, but, if she wished it, he would fight him to the death. Perhaps he would be lucky. Xavier's threats did not frighten him, nor Nicholas's prowess with a sword. He would defend his sister with the last breath in his body, knowing she would do as much for him. It had always been that way between them.

What was she to answer? Nicholas's face told her nothing. Last night she had begged for David's life. Was this his way of giving it to her? The price she already knew, and was as prepared to pay it now as she had been then.

'Yes.' It was done! Now she truly belonged to him.

David's eyes never left her face. Yesterday in his presence she had pleaded for his life, believing, as he did, that he was destined to die. Today that danger had been averted. That meant only one thing to him. She and Nicholas Benedict! Together! With a cry of rage David swung his weapon upwards, only to have it sent spinning out of his grasp as Nicholas anticipated the move and used the last of the strength in his injured arm to deflect the blade and disarm him.

'Kill me,' David growled. 'If I live, I will surely kill you for what you have done.'

'Davie! Oh, Davie, he has done nothing.' Celina ran to him, caught him by the shoulders and looked up into his dark, accusing eyes. 'No matter how hard life became for us, we never lied to each other, did we? I shall not start now. Captain Benedict has not touched me. You have misunderstood.'

She could look at him without flinching and tell him this in all honesty. The relief which flooded into the bearded features told her he believed her.

'Come back into the house, both of you. Go upstairs and get dressed, Celina, then join us in the study,' Nicholas said in quiet tones behind her. Arm in arm, she and David walked back to the house, unaware of the gaping servants who had crept to windows and doors to follow what was going on, oblivious to the look of disappointment on Jean's face as he mounted his horse and rode off in the direction of the drying-sheds. They had eyes only for each other. Watching them, Nicholas felt a pang of envy. Once he and Marianna had been bound by such close ties, until Jean had taken her away from him.

He tried to tell himself it was not this which had made him dislike the man on sight, but the knowledge that he was a liar and a womaniser, seeking feminine company wherever he was, regardless of whether the woman was married or single, or a slave at Paraíso who was too fearful of being sold again to refuse his demands. There had been many of those such incidents until Nicholas had put a stop to it. Now Jean sought his pleasures elsewhere.

Leaning up on tip-toe, Celina kissed her brother's bearded cheeks. The whiskers tickled her mouth.

'You must shave those awful things off; I don't like them. I'll go and dress—I'll only be a little while,' she promised.

'In here.' Nicholas led the way into his study. Xavier came close on his heels, followed by Sulai, carrying a bowl of hot water, bandages and a towel. 'Let the doctor do that,' he intervened as she began to roll back his sleeve. 'He's responsible for it, after all.'

'Will someone find me a knife?' David asked, and Nicholas slipped the one he wore at his side from its leather sheath and held it out to him. A warning look told Xavier to remain at a distance. Trust had to begin between them sometime.

David looked at the sharp blade and into the face of the man who held it. He took it without a word, sliced away the blood-soaked material from wrist to shoulder, and returned it.

'It's a clean wound. Missed the bone by inches,' he remarked, and Nicholas gave a short laugh.

'Nice to know I have an expert opinion. For your information, it hurts like hell!'

'I've seen worse. A hefty swing with a claymore would have taken your arm off, man. There, the bleeding has stopped.' He deftly bandaged the wound and stood back, nodding in satisfaction at his handiwork. 'I haven't lost my touch. I was a good doctor once.'

'I'm going to give you the chance to be so again, if it's what you want. Thank you, Xavier.' Nicholas took the glass of brandy held out to him and swallowed it appreciatively. Never before had he been hurt in such a good cause. His life was beginning to take the strangest of paths, and Celina MacNeill had begun it all. 'One for our friend here, too. Always keep on the good side of a medical man, my father used to say.'

'What are you up to?' David demanded suspiciously. He had not tasted strong spirits in over two years and it burned his throat like fire. He grimaced and refused more. 'Once upon a time that was mother's milk to me, but not any more.'

'In my case it's medicinal,' Nicholas said, sliding off the edge of the desk into his well-worn leather chair in front of it. 'Take these things away, Sulai. I won't be riding anywhere this morning, so you will have to go in my place, Xavier. Check the leaves in number three shed. I noticed yesterday that some of them were too dry. If you think so, move them at once.'

'Yes, Captain. Are you sure . . . ?' The negro hovered by the door in an uncertain manner.

'That our young Scots hothead won't knife me, given the chance? He's had more than one. I'm safe with him.'

'You seem very sure.' David stepped back from him, wary of the seemingly new relationship between them. If any man had tried to kill him, he would not have given him a drink or acted in this cordial fashion. Trust him, Celina had asked. He wanted to, for both their sakes, but he still retained the caution of a man who had been hunted and had learned to trust no one. 'Not every master hereabouts gets such loyalty from his slaves as you do with him—Xavier.'

'He's a free man,' Nicholas returned, and a smile touched his lips at the surprise on David's face. 'I freed him when my father turned this place over to me many years ago. Very few men here are either slaves or indentured to me. They are, when I buy them, but my policy is to give them a year working at Paraíso and then they are freed. Very few leave. I feed and clothe them, give them a place to live. Some marry and raise families. I provide them with everything they want to become as self-sufficient as possible. A contented man works better, don't you agree?'

'They are still tied to you. How can they leave if they don't have the most important thing of all—money?'

'I'm not a benevolent fund,' Nicholas said patiently. 'They can leave any time they wish after a year. Not many do. The life is good here. They profit when Paraíso's sales of tobacco are high, as I do. How long have you been here? Four weeks? More?'

'Five weeks and three days. I know the hours and minutes too,' David said bleakly. He made Paraíso sound paradise indeed, and though he fought against it, he found himself beginning to dwell on the idea. Where else could he go? Do? Here, at least he stood a chance of continuing as a doctor of sorts, and in a year he would be a free man. There was Celina to consider, too.

'I have decided to make an exception in your case. I have already made an error of judgment which needs to be rectified; besides I would like to repay you for your skill. As a doctor, not a swordsman,' he added dryly. 'There are a dozen doctors scattered between here and Kingston. Most of them are more likely to kill than cure. I am willing to gamble that, given the right opportunities and backing, you could set up a sizeable and profitable business in these parts. As of now, you can consider yourself a free man. I'll see to the papers tomorrow.'

'I don't believe you. Is this some game you are playing? I saved the lives of a few sick men and you give me my freedom because of that? It's Celina, isn't it? Somehow I know she is behind this.'

'She knows nothing. Listen to me, MacNeill. Tomorrow you can walk away from here if you so choose. However, I am offering you the opportunity to stand up and be recognised out here. Stay at Paraíso, solely in a medical capacity. The news that I have the one and only decent doctor for miles around will soon bring people flocking to the door. Give yourself six months in which to establish yourself. My sister, as you know, is a cripple. Bedridden. I have it on the best authority that she could walk again. I want her to walk, MacNeill.'

'I can't perform miracles. I haven't even seen the lass close to,' David protested. 'You are crazy.'

'I've been called many things, but never mad,' Nicholas answered, momentary irritation flickering in his eyes. His arm was beginning to throb maddeningly and the brandy had not dulled the pain. He helped himself to another glass. This time David accepted the offer of a second. 'Sit down and listen to me. For six months you are going to stay very close to Marianna, as your sister is doing. Between the pair of you, I think that miracle may come about. I am powerless to do anything . . .'

'Except manipulate other people.'

'Do not presume that this offer of mine in any way puts us on an equal footing, MacNeill.' Nicholas's voice had a dangerous edge to it. 'An assumption of that kind could lead to crossed swords again, and that would be a pity and such a waste of your talent. A dead man cannot practise medicine. Come now, make up your mind, I don't have all day. Accept, and you shall meet my sister this afternoon, after you have made yourself look more respectable so that she'll not think I've let a wild man loose on her. Refuse, and you go back to the fields until your year is up. The choice is yours.'

There was only one answer, David knew. To be free and to practise his skills could not be denied him.

'Celina. What of her?'

'She will remain Marianna's companion, what else? You will work together. She is no longer your problem. Be content with what I have offered you.'

It was in David's mind that Celina, while not having actually lied to him, had concealed the truth to prevent the fight between them continuing. What hold did this man have over her? Had his first suspicions been right, after all? 'I am her brother.'

Nicholas straightened in his chair and looked full into the bearded face. He knew what lurked in David's mind, but said nothing to alleviate his fears. He had done enough. 'In time I shall be more,' was all he said.

'She will not accept you. She has suffered too much at the hands of men like you,' David said harshly. 'You can't imagine what it was like for her in prison. The hell she must have endured in transportation. Women prisoners are easy game, you know that.'

'She will accept me in time.' The confidence in the quiet tones made David uneasy. So sure of himself and of Celina. How had he come to know her so well if he had not laid a finger on her? 'I know how and when to use a velvet glove, MacNeill. But we were not discussing her. What is your answer?'

'You know it. I accept! Damn you, I accept.'

Nicholas ignored the outburst. He had got what he wanted.

CHAPTER
SIX

'PRACTISE MEDICINE. Here at Paraíso?' Celina echoed in disbelief. She had entered the study to find her brother and Nicholas talking as if they were old friends. Her brother rose from the chair in which he lounged at ease, putting aside the glass he held and drew her to a chair nearby him. It was too incredible! Not thirty minutes ago they had been at each other's throats and now he was telling her he was to be Marianna's physician! A free man, able to set up the practice he had always longed for. Free! In his enthusiasm he did not notice the sadness in her eyes. Freedom for him, but not for her. She was shackled until he tired of her, to Nicholas Benedict!

'Aye. A grand opportunity, is it not? And we shall be together,' David said, with a warm smile.

He had accepted the idea all ready, she realised, without considering its drawbacks, or the pitfalls which lay ahead. Free he might be, but he was a stranger in a strange land, among people who might not wish to pay for the services of a transported felon, despite his circumstances now. Was Nicholas really giving him anything. He had his life, which is all she had asked for. Why was it necessary to raise his hopes with an idea which might never bear fruit?

'You appear sceptical at your brother's chances of succeeding. Is he not a good doctor, then?' Nicholas asked, and she looked across to where he sat in indignation.

'Indeed he is!' She retorted without hesitation.

'Then why have you not congratulated him? Are you not pleased?'

'Yes. Of course I am pleased, Davie. It—it was such a surprise, that's all,' she said and hugged him. She was aware of Nicholas's eyes narrowing as he watched them. Why was she so sure he was manipulating them both for reasons of his own? What could he gain from it? David was a fine doctor, but he was used to dealing with country people, fishermen, and ordinary ailments. What could he achieve with Marianna that skilled surgeons and consultants had failed to do?

'Then shall we tell my sister she is to have personal attention from now on?' Nicholas asked, rising. He winced as he did so.

'You should rest that arm,' David said matter-of-factly. 'Or are you not included in my medical care?'

'I dare say there will be another time when I shall be in need of it, but not now; I have too much to do. Besides, it was only a scratch. Thank God you are no swordsman, MacNeill or I would not have come off so lightly.' He rang for Xavier and instructed him to show David upstairs and to fit him out with clothes more suitable to his new position, and then to take him to Marianna's room. As Celina turned to leave, Nicholas stopped her. 'A moment, Celina, before you go.'

He was expecting thanks from her, she thought, as she turned back, but she was mistaken.

'You are not pleased at your brother's change of fortune,' he stated with a frown. 'Why not? Your whole attitude tells me you suspect my motives.'

'How can I, sir, when I do not know them,' she replied.

'My reasons for what I have done are simple enough and have nothing to do with what passed between us last night. I think that is best forgotten, don't you?' He made the incident sound so trivial! For him, perhaps!

He laid no claim to her! She felt quite giddy with relief.

'What a heartless brute you must think me if you believe I would take advantage of a sister's love for her brother,' Nicholas continued. 'I have made too many mistakes of late, Celina. There will be no more, I promise you.' What did he mean by that, she wondered? 'I am convinced Marianna will walk, given time and the right atmosphere. She has shut herself off from people for a long while and must readjust to going out, meeting friends, attending functions and entertaining here again. She will be under great strain in the coming months. I know you will help her in any way you can, but I think it wise for someone with medical knowledge to be on hand also lest she attempt too much too quickly. I want her to walk again. I sincerely believe it is in her power to do so.'

'Surely not,' Celina protested. 'Why should she not have tried before this, if that were so? No one so young and as vital, as you say she was before the accident, willingly lies in bed and loses touch with the world about her. She must have had a reason.'

'None that I know of,' Nicholas answered quickly.

As she followed him upstairs, Celina pondered on the look she had seen in his eyes as he spoke. Now, more than ever, she was convinced that his concern for his sister was not prompted totally by love. Guilt—that was what she had seen. It was as though he were trying to atone for something that had happened in the past, something connected with Marianna and her marriage, perhaps. He did not like Jean—never had, Celina suspected, from the open animosity between them. She had put two and two together from Marianna's declaration that Nicholas left her alone and went off to visit his mistress in Kingston, and that her father loathed the sight of her. It was Celina's belief that the girl had been desperately unhappy and lonely with the prevailing situation, and ready to seize any opportunity to escape from it. Had Jean Leclerc come along then? Had she found in him what she had lost with her brother, the love she had never received from her father?

'She was too young to marry. So ignorant of many things she should have been told,' Nicholas had told her. 'It was I who drove her to the mad decision to elope.' How? Once they had been so close. What had driven a wedge between them?

Marianna sat up in bed, a frosty expression on her pretty face as she listened to Nicholas explaining the presence of David MacNeill in her bedroom. She did not look at all pleased with the news that she was to be taken under his wing and afforded special care every day. Xavier had given him some of the clothes John Benedict had left in his closets. He rarely came back to the house, he was told, and would not miss them.

'Why do you always have to spoil things for me?' she asked sulkily. 'Haven't I had enough of doctors poking and prodding me? None of them did any good. I shall never walk! Why can you not let me go on as I am? I won't let him touch me, so that is an end to it. What are you doing?' Her voice rose sharply as David lifted the covers at the end of the bed and stared at her feet and legs. 'You wretch! Cover me immediately, do you hear?'

'A pity.' He let the covers fall back with a shrug of his shoulders.

'What is?' Marianna glared at the bearded man who faced her. She could see little of his face for all those unkempt whiskers, but the brown eyes that considered her held, to her great indignation, a look that bordered on amusement. 'Who is this man, Nicholas? Where does he come from? Dr Pendennis has always been the family physician. I don't want a change.'

'Pendennis is retiring next month. MacNeill here will be in charge of the family ailments from now on. And anyone relating to the plantation. He will work from here. I thought it best, so that he can be close to you,' Nicholas said, and she caught her breath.

'MacNeill!' she echoed.

'My brother,' Celina replied. 'Until yesterday, when Captain Benedict took me riding with him, I had no idea he was here—or even alive. I thought he had died in England.'

'Another supporter of Charles Stuart!' Marianna declared. 'Are you filling the house with his followers, Nicholas? You expect me to be—be touched by a servant?'

'Your brother has given me my freedom, lass, together with a great opportunity to practise my trade once again. I'm not a butcher and I won't infect you with any disease. On the contrary, you might find my knowledge to be an advantage to you and your condition. I once knew a young boy in similar circumstances. A fisherman. He was injured when his boat overturned in a storm and was washed ashore unconscious. When he came to, he had lost the use of his legs. No one could understand why. There was not a mark on him and he was normal in every other way. A fine lad, he was, about to be married to a local girl. Her father cancelled the wedding; didn't want his daughter saddled to a helpless cripple for the rest of her life. The girl defied him, bless her, married the boy and spent the next two years doing everything she could to help him regain the use of his legs. There wasn't much she could do, of course, except love him.'

'You fool! Love is what put me here,' Marianna cried, and Celina saw Nicholas stiffen visibly. She had touched a nerve, but how?

'I do not think there is any more I can do here, Captain,' David said, turning away from the bed. 'Of course, if you insist, I will make an examination, but I would prefer to do so with the consent of my patient.'

'Tomorrow. And you will allow it, Marianna,' Nicholas told her in an authoritative tone. 'It is for your own good.'

'Everything is always for my own good, isn't it?' Her voice was bitter. Celina had seen her in difficult moods before, but rarely this contrary, and of late her disposition had greatly improved. Jean had brought on this fresh antagonism, she thought angrily. He had undone in a few minutes everything she had achieved since her arrival. 'You, MacNeill. What is a pity?'

'That you will never walk again, but spend your time lying in that bed,' David declared, and the sympathy in his voice stung her. Her husband ridiculed her, this man pitied her, and Nicholas . . . his dark features betrayed nothing. She hurt him so often with her careless words and innuendoes. Would he ever love her as he had once done, or had she destroyed it with her bitterness and guilt?

'I am not confined to bed. Celina and I will go riding in

the carriage. I sit in the gardens and come down to dinner. I am not helpless.'

'Will you ever dance again, show off those trim ankles beneath a beautiful gown?' David's voice suddenly had a hard edge to it. 'I think not. You lack the necessary courage to withstand the pressures I would put upon you if I agreed to help you. It is a pity, because you have such pretty legs.'

'Agreed to help me? You think highly of yourself.'

'I know my limitations, as you seem to know yours. I'll not trouble you longer with my odious company.'

'Wait.' Marianna's voice rang out as Nicholas preceded David to the door. 'This—this boy you spoke of. Did—did he walk again?'

'Aye. It took four years, but one day he got out of bed as though his legs had never been paralysed. A miracle, you might say. The miracle of his wife's love.'

'He was lucky to have her beside him.'

'You have us,' Celina whispered, bending forward to take her hands. 'I can give you little advice, but I shall always be here if you want me. David will be your tutor if only you will trust me, and your brother will give you love—if you will let him. Don't shut any of us out, Marianna.'

Marianna withdrew her hands and sat up. Her lips quivered as she fought a losing battle with herself. To walk again. If only it were possible.

'Very well.' She tried not to sound as if she was acceding to anyone's wishes but her own. 'He may examine me.'

That evening David MacNeill sat across from his sister at the dining-table, together with Marianna, Nicholas and Jean. Marianna had not only allowed herself to be examined, but she had condescendingly given David permission to carry her downstairs.

Celina was pleased to see he had shaved off his growth of whiskers, and Sulai had expertly wielded a pair of scissors on his long hair. He looked his old self again. This was a moment she had never thought could happen again. The two of them together at the same table and, whether she liked it or not, it was all due to Nicholas Benedict. He had not changed for dinner as he usually did. She knew he had gone riding that afternoon and returned an hour later, looking pale and drawn. He had gone direct to his room and stayed there. She had never seen him at a disadvantage before and could not help but feel sorry for him, despite their differences.

'Are we to eat with the hired help every night?' Jean drawled. 'I have no objection to Celina's presence, she is a pleasure to look at, but not this one.'

'Don't be horrid,' Marianna protested. Was he about to make another scene? The news that David was a doctor, and that he would be personally supervising her, had thrown him into a terrible temper and her wrists were still bruised from the rough way he had seized hold of her. She knew he did not want her to walk again, to be part of his life. He had never wanted her, only her money and a comfortable existence. She inwardly shuddered to think of the demands he would make on her if she became well again. 'After all, there is little difference between you.'

Celina caught her breath at the reply, and Nicholas too looked taken aback as he stared down the table at his sister. It was the first time he had ever heard her utter a word against Jean in the whole year they had been married. She was his staunch defender, no matter what he did. Instantly he knew something was wrong between them. But how long had it been this way? Or had it begun only since his sister had begun showing the independent spirit he had loved so much in her as a child? Was Jean afraid that some time in the near future he would have seriously to assume the duties of a husband?

'I think these little outings of yours are overtaxing your strength, my dear,' Jean replied. The smile on his face in no way betrayed the rage seething inside him at her insult. 'Your temper these days is abominable.'

'I am not angry,' Marianna informed him. She must stand up to him or she was lost. 'I was simply drawing a comparison between you and Dr MacNeill.'

'At which I quite correctly take offence. I may work for your brother, but I am also your husband and intend to remain so.' He had everything he wanted at Paraíso, including his freedom. He could come and go at will and he had no intention of changing any of it, or allowing anyone else to do so. Marianna recognised the veiled threat and quickly looked away. Tossing his napkin down on to the table, he rose from his chair. 'I have an engagement which cannot be broken. If you will all excuse me.'

'I want a progress report on the drying first thing in the morning,' Nicholas said, frowning at his rudeness. 'And there are several other little things we need to discuss before I leave. I shall be leaving you short-handed in the house for a few days, but I expect you will manage. I'm taking Sulai and Xavier to Kingston with me. They are getting married.'

'Xavier!' Marianna echoed. 'Why, the sly old devil! I've never once seen him look at Sulai. Not in that way, I mean.'

'You'd be surprised how serious he has been for a long while. A very jealous man is Xavier. Once they are married she'll have to keep a tight rein on him. Anyone who glances twice in her direction is likely to get a knife between the ribs,' Nicholas answered, and he was staring across the room to where Jean stood in the open doorway. The door slammed so fiercely after him that the glasses on the sideboard shook.

Now he knew where he stood, Celina thought, hoping there would be no trouble in that direction. Jean was not the kind of man to relinquish a hold on something he wanted.

'Who will run the house while you are gone?' Marianna asked. 'Surely you cannot expect me . . . I can do a little, but . . .'

'Jean will take care of the plantation side of things,' Nicholas assured her. 'You will not be troubled by it. Not that I expect any difficulties, I shall be away only a few days, after all. I thought Celina would manage. Do you object? She will, of course, come to you if there are any problems, otherwise she acts on her own initiative.'

'What an excellent idea, I'm sure she will manage. Won't you, Celina?'

'If you think me capable,' Celina said, startled.

'I would not have suggested it if I thought otherwise,' Nicholas told her with a smile that wiped a little of the pain from his face. 'Now I, too, am going to leave you. This arm is damned painful.'

'I'll come with you and take a look.' David also rose and the two girls were left alone.

A smile suddenly began to spread across Marianna's face. Celina watched in puzzlement as the other sat deep in thought for several minutes, before exclaiming in an excited tone, 'I think we could do it.'

'Do what?'

'Nicholas's birthday is the week after next. I'm going

to give him a party. I'll draw up a list of guests tonight and you and I will write out the invitations. I'll give them to Xavier to deliver when he reaches Kingston. Sulai shall have the shopping-list. Well? What do you think? Oh, Celina, you should have seen the parties we used to hold here once. When I was a little girl the house was always full of people. I am only now beginning to realise how much I miss it all.'

'I think it's a wonderful idea. He will appreciate it, I know.'

'I owe it to him; I have behaved so badly these past months. We have not really had a party for years, not since long before my accident. Soledad was always inviting people here to dance attendance on her.'

'Soledad? Your stepmother?' Celina asked curiously. It was the first time Marianna had ever mentioned her. 'I hear she was very beautiful.'

'She couldn't have been as beautiful as my real mother. She died giving me birth, and Father hated me for that. He never got over her death. He came and went, leaving the running of Paraíso to Nicholas until he became master, not Father. In the end Father gave it to him, but that was only after Soledad was killed. Compensation for what he had lost, perhaps.'

'Your father or brother?'

'Nicholas, of course. He and Soledad were very close—having an affair, some people suspected. She never let him alone for one moment. I hated her. I was glad when she died.'

'A—a riding accident, wasn't it?' Celina asked cautiously. Nicholas and the lovely Spanish girl his father had married! Two men and the woman they had both hungered for living under the same roof. A dangerous situation for everyone.

'That's what everyone was told. I wouldn't blame Nicholas if he had pushed her over the cliff. She was evil! He looked furious enough to do it when he rode after her that night. I'd been listening to them quarrelling downstairs. The three of them. There had been guests here for the weekend and Father was furious because she had flirted outrageously with so many of the men; with great success, I might add. She laughed in his face and told him he was a boring old man and that she was tired of him and would take her pleasures where she found them. Poor Father. I almost felt sorry for him that night. At last he realised what kind of woman he had put in my mother's place.

'She had begun to tell him how many lovers she had had since they married. "Even your own son could not keep his hands off me when you were away", she had boasted. I heard her quite distinctly,' Marianna said, and Celina gasped aloud. 'Someone slapped her— Father, I think. Nicholas called her a liar, threatened her unless she confessed it was a lie. He sounded like an enraged bull.'

'They were not lovers, then?' How she wished she did not care!

'Or he was desperate to conceal the terrible thing he had done to his own father. I've never been sure.'

'How can you believe your own brother could be so vile?' Celina asked, horrified.

'He is only a man, Celina, and she had a way about her. A dangerous fascination few men could resist. She was only eighteen when Father married her and he was forty-five. Does that help to show you the spell she could weave? He was besotted with her when she first came to Paraíso. It made me ill to watch him.'

'Your brother has a strong character, I am sure.' Why

was she trying to convince herself that Nicholas was innocent of the accusation? Marianna's eyes rested on her thoughtfully, and she prayed she had not given herself away.

'I saw them embracing more than once. Twice I saw them kissing, and he did not look as if he found it distasteful,' she added with a toss of her curls. 'Anyway, it doesn't matter now. She is dead. I heard Nicholas threaten to put his hands round her throat and squeeze the life out of her if she did not tell Father the truth. I saw her face as she ran out of the sitting-room. She was terrified, Celina. I would have been, too, on the wrong end of one of his tempers. She took a horse and rode off. He followed. I saw the way he looked, too. Half an hour later he came back alone and fetched men and lengths of rope. I asked Xavier what had happened and he told me Soledad's horse had thrown her over the cliff by the old house. It's ironical, really. She wanted to live there so much and Father would not give it to her. They were always arguing about its standing empty. She saw herself holding parties there and entertaining her lovers, no doubt.' Marianna reached for the cup of coffee at her fingertips and grimaced to find it was cold. 'I haven't talked this way with anyone for such a long time. Poor Celina, have I bored you?'

'It was all rather sad.'

'Sad. Yes, that is true. Father went away again after the funeral and I thought everything would be the same again for Nicholas and me, but it wasn't. I tried to tell myself the ugly rumours were upsetting him and he would get over it, but he had changed. Withdrawn, curt, even with me. For months I could hardly get a civil word out of him. Soledad was pregnant. Her maid told us. Was it his child, I wondered? Was he mourning the loss

Mills & Boon

Your chance to step into the past and re-live four love stories....

Take four books FREE

Also FREE — a fashionable canvas bag

There's a whole world of romance and history waiting for you...

Take four Masquerade novels FREE with no risk and no commitment.

Discover a world long vanished — a world of chivalry and intrigue, powerful desires and exotic locations, a past that is somehow more real, more gripping, more memorable. Behind the dry, dusty curtain of history are real people, soldiers and statesmen, princesses and serving girls, managing to find true love amid the turmoil that was the Old world all those years ago.

Send today for your Four Free Books, and reserve a Reader Service Subscription for four brand new Masquerade Romances every two months, delivered to your door postage and packing free. And you can enjoy many other advantages:

 No commitment — you receive books for only as long as you want.

 Free newsletter — keeps you up-to-date with new books and book bargains.

 Helpful friendly service from the girls at Mills & Boon. You can ring us anytime on 01-684 2141.

FREE BAG **Our exclusive white canvas tote bag with the Mills & Boon symbol — yours FREE — whatever you decide!**

A subscription to Masquerade Historical Romances costs just £5.00 every two months, but send no money now — these four books are yours to keep — **FREE**. You have nothing to lose — fill in the coupon today.

not only of the woman he loved, but his child, too?'
Marianna shook her head. 'We shall never know. He
never speaks of her. When Jean came into my life it was
suddenly spring, and everything around me was alive
and vital. Someone took an interest in me . . . But that's
another story.' She broke off, realising how close she
had come to divulging the secret she had nursed for the
past year. 'You too, have a way about you, Celina. I talk
too easily to you.'

'I'm glad. Sometimes things, problems, doubts, seem
less troublesome when shared with someone.' How she
wished Marianna had not broken off. She had the feeling
so much would have become clear.

That night, as she lay in bed, her sleep was continually
haunted by a terrible nightmare. She stood on the cliffs
in front of the old house looking down at the broken,
lifeless body of a woman lying on the sands. A few feet
away stood Nicholas, with the look on his face she had
seen before. The day in his study when she had roused
him to anger. Had Soledad, poor unfortunate woman,
seen the face of Blackbeard before she died?

'Come in and close the door, Celina.' She had been
summoned to Nicholas's study again on the morning of
his departure. On her way there, she gave into Xavier's
safe keeping the batch of invitations for the party. They
had taken two days to complete. Both he and Sulai were
taken into Marianna's confidence and sworn to secrecy.
The other servants could be told without fear of a leak,
once Nicholas had sailed for Kingston. 'Come and sit
down.'

David had told her Nicholas's wound had healed well
after an uncomfortable first few days. The colour had
returned once again to his cheeks, she noticed as she

obeyed the order. He always made it sound like an order, not a request, reminding her, perhaps unintentionally, that despite everything, she was still only a servant.

He wore a black shirt, open at the neck, which made his skin look as swarthy as that of a gipsy, hide breeches and long leather riding-boots. It was easy to see why a young girl of eighteen had found him attractive, preferring him to the husband of forty-five, and she was instantly angry with herself for allowing such distracting thoughts to enter her mind in his presence. He had the keen eyes of a hawk and knew when her attention was wandering.

'Marianna seemed in good spirits this morning.' He lit a long cheroot from the box on his desk before turning back to face her. Sunlight slanting through the windows fell across the thick carpet of burnt orange and climbed the skirts of her pale lilac gown. The one she had first worn aboard his ship, he remembered. Yet the girl inside it was different. She looked healthy and had put on some weight, which enhanced the fine bone-structure of her features. Her hair was wound into a thick coil high on the crown of her head, giving her extra height and an elegance he found disturbing. 'Are the two of you planning something special while I am away?'

''Not that I know of, sir.' Celina's heart leapt anxiously. It was not possible he had heard anything, but Marianna's excitement had shown itself, that was all. 'We shall go for carriage-drives, and David has persuaded Marianna to allow him to push her in the wheelchair you bought for her some while back.'

'Has he, now. By God, that's an achievement,' Nicholas ejaculated. 'She took one look at the ugly thing and called me some very unladylike names. He seems to be making progress with her, then?'

'It is too soon to say. It is not something to be rushed, Captain Benedict. The chair first, he thinks; make her accept that, and then perhaps go a stage further if he thinks she is strong enough.'

'Bed to chair. Chair to legs, perhaps? They got on together?'

'They are both as stubborn as mules, but yes,' Celina laughed softly, 'they get on. Marianna has accepted that, for all his occasional gruffness, he is trying to help her.'

'I wish she would believe it of me, too,' Nicholas said, as if to himself. Unexpectedly he asked, 'Why don't you do that more often?'

'Do what?'

'Laugh. It is a lovely sound. Do I still frighten you so much that you cannot be natural in my company?'

She looked at him in astonishment. He had hardly spoken two words to her in the last few days, and now this!

'I assure you I am perfectly natural.'

'Is that why you sit on the edge of your chair as if you suspect I am going to pounce on you suddenly and drag you into my arms?'

'It has happened,' Celina reminded him, a faint blush of colour stealing into her cheeks. Whatever had possessed him to speak to her this way?

'And very enjoyable those occasions were, although you did not think so,' came the amused reply, to heighten her colour still further. 'Enough, Celina, I am only teasing. Don't look so alarmed, besides I have no wish to fight your brother again. He may be an inexperienced swordsman, but he has the damnedest luck. I'll not risk it again. Come here, I have something for you.'

Puzzled, she went to stand in front of the desk. From a drawer he produced a bunch of keys. He was keeping his promise. She was to be in charge while he was away. They were the keys to the house which, if not in his possession, were carried by the trusted Xavier.

'Everything you want is here. Keys for the wine-cellar, my desk here, where you will find money in the top right-hand drawer. More than enough to keep Paraíso going until I return, but I have left a large amount in case of an emergency. You will find out what the rest are for as you go, I dare say. I have given Jean instructions to come to you if there is any trouble in the fields that he cannot deal with. Marianna will have to use her judgment, or the pair of you together. I have no doubt nothing will arise that one of you cannot cope with. I leave Paraíso in your hands, then, Celina MacNeill. Take good care of it for me, I am very fond of this old place. You . . .' he hesitated, and she saw he was hesitant to continue.

'Will I what, Captain Benedict?'

'You will be here when I return, won't you?'

For a full minute she stared at him, not understanding. The money—the keys to the house! She could take anything of value and be gone. David too.

'Do you think I would run away and leave Marianna? How could you?' she cried angrily and threw the bunch of keys down on to the polished mahogany. 'Take them back. I won't accept them.'

With narrowed eyes, Nicholas picked them up and came round to where she stood. He took her unresisting hand and pressed the keys into it.

'You will, and you will be mistress here until I come back. If you are not here, Celina, I want you to know I shall come after you and I shall bring you back.' For all his softness of tone, the words chilled her, and then he smiled, and the threat might never have been uttered. He would come after her, though, she knew it.

'I am neither a thief nor a coward. Your money will be here when you return, and so shall I.'

'Good. You will not regret that decision, I promise. Be what you were, Celina. Take this chance and be yourself again. Believe in yourself again.'

Celina raised her head and stared at him, asking with sudden boldness, 'Will you ever believe in me, Captain Benedict, or am I to spend the next seven years with your eyes for ever following me, suspecting everything I do, everyone I speak to? A bird cannot fly free and high if it is tethered to the ground by a long rope, and that is how I feel. I can go so far, but no further lest I displease you.'

'Make me believe in you,' Nicholas murmured. His hand was still clasping hers. She felt his fingers tighten for a moment before he released her and stepped back. She left the room feeling as though she had wandered unknowingly into a quicksand.

The day after Nicholas's departure, David took Marianna for a picnic, and Celina was left to acquaint herself with the routine of the house. The servants had all been told she was in charge, and were most helpful with answers to her many questions. None of them appeared to resent her temporary position, and she forgave the few of them who actually found it amusing. It was natural for Nicholas's action to provoke some gossip, she told herself, and pretended not to notice the smiles and knowing looks.

She went through the house, trying out every key, and by the end of the day knew where all, but one, belonged.

'That one,' Marianna said, examining the small ornate key Celina gave her. 'Yes, it's the key to the old house. Nobody ever goes there now and Nicholas keeps it locked. Some of the beams are rotten and could be dangerous, he said. Stop playing housekeeper and come and help me make up this menu. It has to be something really splendid. If everyone who has been invited comes, there will be over a hundred guests.'

Three days later, after alterations and long hours of deliberation which involved not only Marianna and Celina, but David too and the cook and two of the kitchen-maids, it was decided there should be a cold buffet comprising roast chickens, turkeys, sides of ham and beef, all with the appropriate sauces and accompanying side-dishes. Fresh seafood—prawns and shrimps, lobsters and crayfish and crabs. Celina began to feel hungry just listening to the final completed menu being read out. The cook was to make a birthday cake filled with cream and fresh strawberries, and dozens of small cakes would be baked, iced, sugared, filled with a variety of mouth-watering delicacies. There was to be a massive punch-bowl and champagne.

David carried Marianna down to the ample cellars where the wine was stocked, and the three of them stood in awe of the racks of bottles, mostly inches thick in dust, which lined the walls.

'Where did all this come from?' Celina asked, selecting a bottle at random. 'Look, David. Vintage French claret. How do you come by this when we are at war, Marianna?'

'I'm afraid Nicholas has some very peculiar friends. I'm sure most of this is contraband.'

'Friends—like the "Fox"?' Celina asked, and saw Marianna's face grow pale in the candlelight.

'I've never heard of him. Bring the light, will you? We must find out how much champagne we have.'

As she followed, Celina knew she had lied. Another secret Paraíso had not yet yielded up to her.

Despite Jean's belligerent attitude, David managed to keep his temper whenever he appeared unannounced in Marianna's bedroom to intrude into their conversation. Celina marvelled at his patience. He always quietly withdrew, not returning until Jean had gone again. Scenes between Marianna and her husband were growing commonplace. So, too, were the bruises to be seen on her arms and wrists. Celina was quickly cut short when she attempted to ask what had happened, and she knew that her brother had no better luck.

The wheelchair Nicholas had brought to the house was resurrected from the attic where it had been taken after Marianna's refusal to use it, cleaned and brought to the bedroom. Celina could have cried with joy when she climbed unaided from the bed and pulled herself into it. Marianna had been practising at night when she was alone, and Celina had found out quite by accident. She was determined to make the supreme effort. How proud Nicholas would be of her when he returned!

In another day, perhaps two, he would be home. Her heart leapt unexpectedly as she walked along the cliffs one afternoon. His ship would come round the headland, and she would be able to see it hours before it actually dropped anchor in Benedict's Bay. The party preparations were in full swing and the house was a hive of activity. She had stolen a few minutes to herself while Marianna rested in her room.

She felt a twinge of shame as she walked along the floral mile, as she had named it, towards the sea, for she realised that she had given no thought to Craig Tor and

Scotland for many days. She was beginning to make her life around David and Marianna and Paraíso. She had discovered a short cut which brought her out to the bay in half the time, making it possible for her to walk here often without spending too much time away from the house, although she knew Marianna was in good hands during her brief absences.

The old house stood out in front of her, neglected, beckoning. Her fingers touched the keys in her pocket and came away as if they were suddenly red hot. She dared not! Nicholas had locked the house because it was dangerous. Besides, if he learned she had gone there without his permission . . . ! Why did she sense that this house held the answers to so many of her questions?

She looked towards the sea and caught her breath. There was a ship anchored in the bay. It did not belong to Nicholas Benedict. This one was heavily armed and reminded her of the ship which had intervened to save them from the French man o'war. A privateer anchoring in Benedict's Bay? What was it Marianna had said? 'I'm afraid Nicholas has some very peculiar friends.' But he was away from Paraíso, and she had seen no strangers the last few days. Was this the 'Fox' 's ship? If so, where was he?

Her gaze was drawn back to the house. It looked deserted, but the gates stood ajar. Someone was inside. It was her responsibility to find out who it was, since she had been left in charge!

The perfume of the last roses hung in the air as she walked slowly along the weed-strewn path to the huge brass-studded door. A board creaked beneath her feet as she mounted the veranda steps and tried the handle. The door did not yield. It was still locked. No one had come ashore after all, she thought in relief. Having come

this far . . . one glimpse inside could not be so
wrong . . .

The key turned easily in the lock and she realised it
had been recently oiled. How strange, if no one came
here? She stepped into a large entrance hall, dark with
shadows, for all the rooms beyond had the windows
shuttered. A shaft of sunlight followed her, creeping
across the dusty floor, chasing spiders back into their
webs with the sudden bright light. Her footsteps echoed
on the wooden floor as she crossed to the first door and
found herself standing in a pleasantly furnished sitting-
room. Only a few pieces of furniture had dust-covers
over them, the rest had been left untouched. It was a
mixture of English and French styles, she saw. Velvet-
covered chaise-longues with inches of grime on them.
Ornate mantel clocks and a tall slender cased regulator.
Multi-coloured cushions piled high on a couch placed in
the curved window area. A carved oak dresser stood
beside a Queen Anne walnut card-table with cabriole
legs. Resplendent against one wall was a writing-table
from the Louis XIV period, the beautiful ebony and
boulle marquetry almost obscured by dust. She would
have given anything to have a duster in her hands.

'What a waste,' she whispered sadly. 'Such lovely
things.' The room cried out for attention, but received
none. This was the house Soledad Benedict had so
desperately wanted and had been refused. 'I would like
it, too.'

Nothing happened to make her aware that anyone
else was present, but all at once she knew she was not
alone. Her heart in her mouth, she spun about and found
a man standing in the doorway behind her.

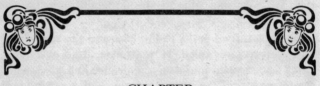

CHAPTER
SEVEN

'WHO ARE YOU?' Celina demanded. She was in charge at
Paraíso and he had no business here. His legs were
encased in high sea-boots which reached well above the
knees of well-worn breeches. The shirt he wore was
creased, one of the lace ruffles at the sleeves, torn. Over
this he had on a leather waistcoat. A common seaman,
was her first impression, drawn to the empty house by
curiosity, as she had been. But there was something
about the man's features that gave her second thoughts.

It was a face she could describe only as kind, despite
its weather-beaten appearance. She realised that brown
eyes were surveying her with as much frankness as hers
were him.

'Your name, sir,' she repeated stubbornly. 'You have
no right to be here.'

'No more have you, my pretty. Who are you to
demand my name in such high-handed tones?' The voice
was cultured and very English.

'I am Celina MacNeill. Captain Benedict has left me
in charge while he is away.' She had supplied the information before realising the ease at which he immediately put her.

'You? Little liar. Nicholas would not leave a slip of a
girl to take care of Paraíso. Who are you? What are you?
With that accent I'd say you are an émigrée or an

indenture. Which is it?'

'That is none of your business,' Celina gasped.

'Make it mine, then.' The man stepped towards her, his face cold and unfriendly. 'Nicholas allows no one to come here, I know that. What are you looking for?'

'Nothing.' Celina took a step away from him. He was blocking her escape to the door. She pulled the bunch of keys from her pocket and held them out. 'Look! I have spoken the truth, how else would I have these? Captain Benedict has taken Xavier and Sulai with him, so there was no one else except Marianna, and she is incapable in her condition. If you say you know the captain, then you also know about her. And why she could not manage to run the house.'

'Because she is a cripple. There is little I don't know about the inhabitants of Paraíso, pretty lass. You are new, though.'

'Captain Benedict engaged me as companion to his sister.' She balked at telling this stranger she had been bought like a piece of merchandise. 'Your ship prevented us from being attacked by a Frenchman on the way from Antigua. You are the man Captain Benedict calls the "Fox", are you not?'

A smile touched the man's face, dispelling the coldness there, although the eyes remained a trifle wary as they continued to study her.

'He has spoken of me to you?' He sounded surprised.

'He knew your ship, and I asked him how. He said you are a privateer. He appeared to be quite pleased you were back in these waters. I realised then that you were his friend. Besides,' a mischievous smile lit up her features, 'who else could keep his wine-cellars stocked so well?'

The man threw back his head and bellowed with

laughter which echoed around the room.

'I like you, Celina MacNeill. You are no danger to me. Come away from here and have a glass of wine with me. I should like to talk further with you.'

'No. I must not stay,' Celina said quickly as he turned away. Dearly as she would have liked to stay and wander through the house and learn more of this strange man, she dared not linger. He seemed harmless, and he was Nicholas's friend, but . . .

'Why not? Even a companion has a little spare time to herself, does she not? And the master is away . . .'

'I would not like Captain Benedict to think I have gone behind his back in coming here.'

'But you have! Afraid of him, are you?'

'No! Well, yes,' Celina admitted with reluctance. 'I find him a strange man. Difficult to understand and totally unpredictable.'

'Do you, now? That's interesting. These past years I've thought him totally predictable. Still, the lad was badly hurt . . .'

'I know. I mean . . . I've heard the talk.' Celina naturally assumed that he was referring to Soledad and the rumoured affair between them.

'What kind of talk?'

'About Captain Benedict and . . . Oh, they were only rumours and too awful to repeat.'

'Nicholas and his stepmother. The lovely, treacherous Soledad.' The 'Fox' supplied the answer for her. So he knew about her, too! A very old friend indeed. 'So the mud still clings, no wonder the lad feels so bitter. Do you believe it?'

'I—don't know,' Celina answered hesitantly.

'Do you think Nicholas capable of stealing his father's wife?'

'Yes, I think it possible. I gather she was very beautiful.'

'Not as lovely as his real mother.'

'That is what Marianna thought.'

'You seem to know a great deal despite your short acquaintance with the family, and I think you have a reason for believing the worst of him, but I'll not ask you what it is. Not now, anyway. Stay a while longer. Would you like to see over the house?'

'Oh, yes. But I mustn't . . .' Why did he have to ask her that?

'Nonsense, you shall and you will have that glass of wine with me.'

'What are you doing here? Does Captain Benedict know?' Celina asked, following him out into the hall again. Her skirts dragged in the dust, leaving a wide line behind her.

'I always anchor my ship in the bay. He gets to know it is there, one way or another. He allows me to stay here if I wish. There are times when the solitude appeals to me. And to you, I think?'

'I think it is a great shame to leave such a place unlived-in, for the flowers to grow wild and the weeds to choke the life from them,' she declared, following him upstairs. It was a narrow staircase, so different from the one at the other house. The banisters had once been polished wood inlaid with tiny pieces of bright green marble. Bright sunlight greeted her as they reached the next floor. A corridor ran the whole length of the house, giving access to perhaps a dozen rooms. All the shutters had been thrown open, and she gave a distressed cry at the sight of peeling paint, doors hanging from their hinges, broken windowpanes and everywhere furniture covered in dust. On a chair in front of her a mother cat nursed four newly-born kittens and looked up warily to watch her pass.

'Why does this old house touch your heart, Celina MacNeill?' the 'Fox' asked curiously. 'It is fit only for ghosts to live in. Are you not happy in the new Paraíso? It is so much larger and more comfortable. Do you not have everything you want there?'

'Yes. I cannot explain how I feel. When I first saw it as I came up from the bay it reminded me of home. The house I was born in was on a headland. Every room was alive with the sound of the sea.'

'Like this?' He threw open a window beside him and immediately she could hear the loud cry of a seagull as it swooped low over the roof and the deep booming sound of the rollers crashing onto the rocks along the shore. She became aware of him watching her amusedly. 'Home, you say. How did your family fare after Charles Stuart turned tail and left others to pay the price for the failure of his dreams?'

'He did not flee,' Celina retorted hotly. 'He was no coward. My brother and I are alive. The rest of my family is dead. My home a ruin. The English were very thorough.'

'How did you escape, then?'

'We did not.' She spoke without thinking and the brown eyes gleamed in such a way that she suddenly found herself thinking of Nicholas Benedict. 'Neither of us left Scotland willingly, sir. We were transported as indentured servants. My brother has just been appointed personal physician to Marianna.'

'And Nicholas bought you, then. In Antigua.' The man gave a long, low whistle. 'I find that astounding and totally out of character, but then you describe him these days as unpredictable. The advice I gave him has been well taken, it seems.'

'Advice?' Celina echoed. 'I don't understand.'

'I am only now beginning to,' he chuckled and she knew she was not to be enlightened.

He showed her all the rooms. Four bedrooms, each with a sitting-room and small adjoining antechamber. They were not large, but the view from every window was breathtaking. He laughed as she opened every window in every room and brought in the sounds of the sea and the wind and the birds. She had fallen in love with the place, he told her, and she could not deny it. She had known, that first day she saw it, that if she ever set foot inside she would want to live here.

'Why was it so cruelly abandoned?' she asked. They sat in one of the sitting-rooms. The walls had once been the blue of the sky, the curtains rich velvet with golden cords, the furniture delicate brocade chairs and matching sofa. A jacket was tossed across the latter, and through the open door she could see that the covers had been stripped from the bed and replaced by fresh ones. This man certainly know his way about the house and made himself very much at home, she mused, as he reached for the decanter of wine at his fingertips and poured some into two wafer-thin crystal goblets. Not wishing to offend him, she accepted one.

'Try it,' he insisted and she tasted it. It was sweet and full bodied. She smiled approval. 'It came off the man o'war I chased that day. The French always live well wherever they are. The holds were full of the stuff. Nicholas shall have two dozen cases by this evening, but you had better let me tell him of their arrival. He would not be too pleased to know you have been here, and I like your company too much to have him spoil the prospect of another visit.'

'I must not come again.'

'Nonsense. You have achieved today what the sunlight failed to do. I was feeling quite morose until you appeared. The place does that to be sometimes. I still think Elizabeth walks around here. She, too, must feel unhappy at the way it has been neglected. You asked why it was abandoned? That was Soledad, the second mistress of Paraíso. It was not grand enough for her to live in, and so Captain John built a new house. Later, though, she wanted it for herself, but it was too late. Love had died in him and he gave her nothing. He preferred to see the place rot than have her entertain her . . . friends here.' The hesitation was not lost on Celina. If he was a close friend of Nicholas, a confidant perhaps, he would know the truth about the rumours. How she wished she had the courage to ask him.

'I must go.' Celina rose to her feet, aware of time passing and that she might be missed. 'Thank you for letting me see the house.'

'I think she was pleased to see you. Come again, Celina MacNeill.'

'No, that is not possible.'

'You will come. You will not be able to help yourself. You'll see.' The 'Fox' smiled at her from his chair. 'I shall be here for a few days. Come back tomorrow and maybe I'll have found a pretty bauble to grace that lovely throat of yours.'

Celina coloured, embarrassed that he considered she could be bought. Was the stigma which accompanied an indentured servant to cling to her for ever? She would not return. At least not until he had gone. But she did, the very next day, as he had suggested, drawn by a force too strong to resist.

*   *   *

'It is too bad of Nicholas to stay away this long,' Marianna protested as the three of them went over final details for the party. 'His birthday is in four days! What if he doesn't come back in time? I shall never speak to him again. I suppose his lady-friend is making the time pass so quickly for him that he has not given us a second thought.'

'Why should he?' David asked, settling back in his chair. He was at ease in her company these days, Celina noticed. 'He doesn't know what you are planning, does he?'

'No, but he still said a few days, not a week,' Marianna insisted. 'How many guests can we put up in the house if necessary, Celina?'

'If the women do not mind sharing rooms with friends and the men do likewise, about forty. There are at least eight unused rooms in this house and all are potential bedrooms. If more are needed, my sitting-room can be used and we could also erect a marquee on the lawn.'

'What a good idea. You have thought of everything. Oh, Celina, what would I have done without you? I have done very little myself, I have been so tired.'

'I did warn you about over taxing your strength,' David said gently. 'A little each day, not all at once, or you will end up in that bed for a week on my orders.'

'You are a bully.' Marianna pouted. 'Does he bully you too, Celina?'

'Often,' she laughed, and David spun round on her, his eyes full of amusement.

'There's only one man in this house capable of bullying my sister, isn't there, Celina?'

He meant Nicholas! How had she given herself away? Or had it been a shrewd guess? She ignored the question in his eyes and began gathering up the papers strewn across the bed.

'I promised to go through the menu again with Cook before dinner tonight. I've never seen so much food in all my life. The cupboards are bulging, and the sauces she was making yesterday smelled delicious. I had to taste them.'

'She always smacked my fingers and shooed me out of the kitchen,' Marianna declared.

'She did the same to me. I—I might go for a walk before dinner if you do not need me for anything.'

'No, I don't think so. Where do you go to on these walks? Every day you seem to disappear for an hour or two?' Marianna looked at the other girl curiously. Had Celina found herself a beau from among the Highlanders working the plantation? She would have to approve him, of course, if it was serious. And so would Nicholas. Celina was not just anyone. She could make a good marriage for herself if she chose. It might be an idea to mention what was in her mind to David MacNeill first. He was her brother, after all. Twice Jean had seen her slipping into the old house. Marianna knew he had told her only because he was jealous, no—annoyed, that she had not been tempted to take up with him. He had made no secret of the fact he had wanted her. Since Marianna had made the mistake of letting him know his unfaithfulness was no secret to her, he delighted telling her of his escapades—even with Sulai—and there was nothing she could do, because she could not leave her bed. One day . . . one day soon, she would surprise him. On the very first day she stood alone and unaided and took that first precarious step, she would tell him to leave Paraíso for ever.

'Nowhere,' Celina answered quickly. Too quickly,

Marianna thought. She was more convinced than ever that Celina had found herself a man. 'Just in the forest. It is pleasant and I enjoy walking. You don't mind, do you?'

'Of course not. Go along and enjoy your—walk.'

Had she been seen, Celina wondered, as she made her way towards the cliff-top house, and decided she had not. Marianna obviously knew nothing of the 'Fox''s visits there. Once or twice she had been near to telling her of the encounter, but remembering her denial that she knew anyone of that name, Celina remained silent. Was he not only a privateer, but, as so many of those men were, inclined to piracy if pickings became lean? Her footsteps slowed. How strange she should recall to mind that phrase. 'Are pickings lean on the Caribbean these days?' the man called Lester had remarked to Nicholas in Antigua. A strange thing to say to a man who ran a tobacco plantation. It was more in keeping for the 'Fox', not Nicholas. There was a connection somewhere which seemed to indicate a closer relationship between the two men, but it escaped her.

'Come in, pretty lass, and sit down.' The man was waiting for her, as he always was. He gave her the impression that he not only liked her company, but looked forward to her visits. Nicholas's return would curtail those. She was sorry in a way. Despite the mystery about him, the knowledge he might not be what he seemed, she had grown to like him too. As usual, a glass of wine was waiting for her. She reached for it with a smile.

'You spoil me.'

'And why not? Does no one else do so?'

'There is no one, except my brother.'

'Brothers and sisters always take each other for

granted. Rather like husbands and wives do in time,' the 'Fox' retorted with a grimace. 'A young woman like you should have men dancing attendance on her, showering her with compliments.'

'No!' Celina said, so sharply, that he broke off and looked at her in astonishment. 'I don't want that. The only men I've ever known since leaving Scotland have been ruffians, heartless creatures who preyed on the miseries of someone like myself . . . the helplessness . . . the loneliness . . . because I was at a disadvantage, they thought . . .'

'Are you including our friend Nicholas among them?' came the amused question, and she blushed beneath his scrutiny.

'No. He—he does not count. I belong to him. I'm just an addition to Paraíso, that's all.'

'If he thinks of you that way, he's blind, and if he lets you go, he's a damned fool! What of these others . . . who were they?'

Celina looked into the face before her and discovered an expression of great concern on it and gentleness in the brown eyes. Why he should profess to care, she did not know, or why she should unburden herself with the nightmare of that trip again, but she did, and he listened in silence until she had finished.

'If any one of my crew acted that way with a woman, I'd have hung him from the yardarm,' the 'Fox' sneered. 'You've had a rough time, lass, and it's marked you. That's a pity. This world can be a lonely place with no one to trust. Believe it, I know. Let me put a smile back on your face. Come and see what I have brought for you.'

Mystified, Celina followed him across to a small bureau. From a top drawer he took out a faded velvet box and snapped back the lid. Celina found herself looking down at an emerald pendant with earrings to match. One single stone made up the pendant. It was set in gold, on a long twisted rope of gold.

'How beautiful!' she exclaimed.

'They once belonged to a woman I was fond of. I've never found another worthy of wearing them.' He closed the lid again, replaced them in the drawer and took out a leather pouch. On to the top of the desk he tipped the contents—rings, bracelets, earrings, necklaces. Celina's eyes grew wide at the array of priceless gems. Rubies, pearls, diamonds, sapphires. 'Choose anything you like.'

'I cannot.' She drew back, instantly suspicious of such generosity, and the 'Fox' smiled sadly.

'Poor Celina, so afraid to trust even this harmless old man. Take something, I insist. A token of my gratitude for your visits. They have meant a great deal to me. I find you refreshing. A breath of spring in my fading autumn years.'

He was not old, Celina thought, no more than fifty-six or -seven, even though his hair was totally grey. It gave him a most distinguished appearance. Yet today she thought how tired he sounded and, not wanting to spurn the gesture, moved back to the bureau. How could she choose from such a collection! A large silver locket, set with rubies and pearls, caught her eyes. She liked it because the stones were arranged to make the first letter of her name.

'I should not, but if you insist, may I have this?'

'The rich fire of rubies and the purity of pearls. You have not disappointed me. Most women, especially your age, would have chosen diamonds, sapphires, big sparkling stones to show off to their friends. But then you have no friends, have you, Celina MacNeill?'

'I have my brother and Marianna and—and I have you,' Celina replied, slipping the gift into her pocket. 'Will you be staying for Captain Benedict's birthday? We have a surprise party planned for him.'

'So that's the reason for all the activity,' the man declared. 'No, I think not. Open a bottle of our French claret for him. He'd prefer that to my company.'

'I thought you and he were friends?' Celina said, taken aback by the statement. 'You are, aren't you?'

The 'Fox' considered her for a long moment before he slowly nodded.

'Aye, lass, and much more. Get you gone before you are missed. Wear that bauble at the party, make some handsome young man notice you.'

'I dare not. He—Captain Benedict—would want to know where it came from. He would not be at all pleased to know I have been seeing you here, alone.'

'Would he not? He is the only one allowed the pleasure of your company, is he? I envy him. Goodbye, pretty lass. When I have gone, find time to come here sometimes if you can. You will always be welcome. I promise no one, not even Nicholas, will prevent it if you wish to do so.'

But he would be gone and Nicholas would never allow it, much as she wanted to return, Celina thought, as she returned to the house for dinner. What an odd character. During none of their conversations had he ever volunteered his real name, and she knew that, had she asked, he would have refused it. She knew as little about him as on the first day they had met. But she was glad they had. Whatever the 'Fox' was, privateer or pirate, whoever he was, she considered him a friend.

'I trust your walk has not tired you? You look a little

flushed?' Jean remarked, coming up behind her as she mounted the steps to the front door. She had seen him coming through the gardens and deliberately pretended otherwise. She found his treatment of Marianna hateful and his continued attempts to seduce her distasteful and at times, frightening. Nothing she said or did dissuaded him.

'It is a warm day.' She brushed aside the arm he held out and preceded him inside. He chuckled as he bent his head close to hers.

'And it is quite a long way to the old house, *n'est ce pas*?'

She ran upstairs with his hateful laughter ringing in his ears. He had seen her. He knew she had been meeting someone, his tone of voice betrayed that. What if he told Nicholas, made it sound as if she had been sneaking off to meet—a lover? That's what he would think, and he would believe Jean because he mistrusted her.

Marianna was not upstairs. Her maid told Celina that she and David had accompanied a neighbour to the stables. He had brought several horses at her request for her to see. It was her birthday-present-to-be for her brother. Carefully avoiding the sitting-room where she could hear Jean remonstrating with one of the servants because dinner was to be an hour late, she slipped out to join them.

Four new horses stood in the stalls being expertly inspected by her brother. He was in his element here, she thought. He stared curiously at her red cheeks for a moment, but did not make a comment.

'What do you think? Marianna likes the bay. I prefer the one with white stockings. A good horse that, he would breed well.'

So he called her Marianna now! Jean would not like to

hear that. She inspected the new arrivals but, being no expert on horseflesh, chose one for purely personal reasons. It was a stallion, with a flaming red coat, and eyes as black as jet.

'Why that one?' Marianna asked in surprise. 'He is rather magnificent, but Nicholas already has a fine blood stallion.'

'He reminds me of . . .' She broke off, realising what she had been about to say, and they both looked at her expectantly.

'Well,' David insisted. 'Tell us.'

'He has such wicked eyes. He reminds me of Captain Benedict,' Celina said lamely, and his face split into a wide grin. Marianna smothered her laughter in her hands for several minutes, but it became too great and tears came into her eyes.

'Oh, Celina, he shall have that one and I shall tell him why. I agree, he does have Nicholas's eyes. I would never have noticed it. I wasn't looking for anything like that. I've left Mr Dennison in the study drinking Nicholas's best port. He's very partial to port. We may be able to have this animal at a reasonable price.'

Nicholas Benedict returned home early the next morning. He found the house perfectly organised and being run as efficiently as when he had left it. Celina returned his keys, assured him that nothing amiss had taken place, and escaped quickly upstairs to sort through the mass of replies Xavier had brought back with him. Sulai, too, had completed her errands and returned with every item Marianna had requested. Nicholas had been told only that his sister required the things for the house and he had asked no further questions. How happy the woman looked, Celina thought as they sat together, discussing what was to take place in a few days. If only Jean would leave her alone now. To continue pestering Sulai would bring him into conflict with Xavier. The outcome, she suspected, would be most unpleasant for one of them.

There were extra sheets and bedding to be aired, and warming-pans cleaned and placed in each room. Celina spent the whole of that day supervising preparations for the guests, relieved that Nicholas had immediately gone on an inspection of the plantation with Jean, who complained loudly at being dragged from the house before he had breakfasted.

The day before his birthday, as they all sat at dinner, Nicholas commented on the large amount of cooking being done since his return. 'Are guests expected that I know nothing about?' he asked, looking down the table to where his sister sat. Marianna looked up at him, her face as innocent as a day-old babe.

'Guests? Why, not that I know of. Would you like to invite some people, Nicholas? I am sure I could cope with just a few for a weekend. Perhaps half a dozen.'

'That would be nice. Perhaps in a week or two if you still feel like it. And the smell of cooking that has invaded every corner of this house?'

'Oh, that. Celina gave me some Scottish recipes that her family once used. I am so tired of the same old food week after week that I gave them to cook to experiment with.'

'Celina does very well for herself these days, doesn't she?' Jean remarked, and David instantly bristled. The two men had come close to blows on more than one occasion over his treatment of Marianna, who could no longer hide the fact that when her husband was drunk, which was most nights since Sulai had married, he came to her room and took out his spite on her. Each morning there were fresh bruises. She had refused to tell Nicholas, and David had taken it upon himself to tackle the man. It had taken all Celina's strength to part them as tempers rose.

'I see no reason for that tone, Jean. She has proved herself most competent,' Nicholas answered, frowning slightly at the dissension this man carried with him everywhere he went. He was fast disrupting the every-day routine which made the running of the plantation so effective. He had heard rumours of beating among the negroes, but no one had come forward in answer to his call for confirmation. They were all afraid of Jean Leclerc's devious methods of reprisals against anyone who crossed him. Before much longer, Nicholas knew, things must come to a head between them. He could hold back, for Marianna's sake, no longer.

'I have no doubt she is competent in everything she does,' Jean said, his eyes narrowing as they encountered Celina's apprehensive expression. Was he about to di-vulge her visits to the old house? He kept her waiting in suspense for a full minute before he laughed and left the room. He always left before the meal was over. No one knew where he went and did not care enough to ask. As always when he had gone, the atmosphere returned to normal and lighthearted conversation returned. Nicholas might suspect that something was going on un-der his very nose, but he was not sure, and tomorrow . . . His birthday present had been carefully hidden in an unused barn half a mile away, and a young lad set there day and night to guard the valuable acquisition. How would he respond when Marianna told him what Celina had said? She was determined on it, and there was nothing Celina could say to make her change her mind.

Nicholas did not think it strange when Marianna voiced her intention of retiring early, but he did look annoyed when Celina turned down his invitation to remain and have her coffee and port with him in another room. With a shrug of his shoulders, he dismissed her, and retired to his study with Xavier.

The day dawned overcast, with dark clouds threatening rain. Marianna groaned at the dismal sky, for it was intended to have a picnic lunch in the woods behind the house. An hour later, the sun broke through the cloud, and she brightened as quickly as the weather. They decided to go ahead as planned.

'What are you doing down here this early?' Nicholas looked up in surprise as David carried her into the dining-room. 'Is today special that you decide to break-fast with me?'

'Of course it is, silly. Come here. Let me wish my brother a very happy birthday.'

'So you didn't forget, you little minx.' He kissed her affectionately before looking up into the two smiling faces behind him. 'Something is going on, isn't it?' His eyes searched David's face. He was hoping for the best kind of news, Celina realised.

'I have arranged a real birthday for you, to make up for last year and all those other times when I was so childish,' Marianna said happily. 'I was so afraid you would not come back in time.'

'Where would I be, but Paraíso, on such an occasion,' Nicholas returned. A momentary frown creased his brows and Celina realised he had seen the dark smudges on his sister's wrists. Not now, she thought anxiously. Don't spoil everything for her now! 'Tell me, then, I am dying with curiosity.' She silently breathed a sigh of

relief. She did not realise it, but Nicholas had noticed the
tension in her face. Later he would ask why.

'I—we, I cannot take full credit for anything. We did it
between us,' Marianna said. 'We are going to have a
picnic lunch in the woods. Over sixty people replied to
my invitations. Xavier delivered them for me; wasn't I
clever to think of that? And Sulai did extra shopping.
You didn't guess for one moment, did you?'

'I certainly did not . . . I wondered a little about those
beautiful smells coming from the kitchen, though. Is it to
be as mouth-watering as it smelled?'

'Those? They are for tonight. Tonight, Nicholas
Benedict, we are going to have the grandest party
Paraíso has ever seen. You just wait until you see what
has been arranged for you. Now, pay attention and I
shall tell you the schedule.'

'Am I not allowed to do what I please on my birthday?' Nicholas asked in mock indignation.

'After all our hard work? Certainly not, you will do as
you are told and enjoy yourself,' Marianna laughed.
'You must go and change directly and be ready to greet
your guests. I have invited everyone I thought you might
want to see, including Joanna, but she has declined the
invitation. Have you quarrelled?'

'Joanna and I never quarrel,' Nicholas replied good-
humouredly. 'She has other plans which cannot be
broken, that's all. Important plans.'

'More important than being with you?' Marianna
looked at him closely. 'What are you smiling about? Is
there something I should know? You haven't—you
haven't asked her to marry you?'

'Would you mind if I had? I thought you liked her.
You both got on well the last time I brought her here.'
Celina felt herself grow cold at his words. She had never

thought the relationship to be that intense. 'She likes you, I know.'

'Yes, I like her. Oh, Nicholas, do tell me.'

'You shall hear everything in good time, I promise. However, I will set your mind at rest on one thing. I am intending to get married. It's time I settled down, don't you think? Now, let me hear more of this birthday treat. The surprises should be for me today, not you.'

'We shall take coffee and cakes and little nibbles . . . you know the things women like to eat while they gossip, in the sitting-room while you and the men gather in the study and get rid of all your boring old business discussions. That way, the servants can deal with the luggage and sort out the accommodation. If everyone stays overnight, we shall need the marquee Celina suggested.'

'You seem to have thought of everything between you,' Nicholas mused.

'At eleven, there will be carriages waiting to take us all on a picnic in the woods. Everything is prepared. When we come back, we can rest before the evening. And then—' Marianna's face lit up with excitement. He could not remember the last time she had looked so interested in anything, Nicholas thought, and wondered what miracle Celina and her brother had wrought to bring about such a change in her. 'There is to be a cold buffet laid in the dining-room, extending out on to the terrace. And music for dancing. Celina has found two of her countrymen who have fiddles and those funny bagpipes, and I'm sending a cask of wine and some food to the field-hands to celebrate, too. Why not, Father always did . . .' Her voice trailed off and she looked discomforted. Celina had never heard her mention her father before. He was a part of her life she preferred to forget.

'He would be pleased that the gesture is still remembered,' Nicholas said quietly, and kissed her again. 'Marianna, what a day I shall have. Thank you, my sweet. I shall enjoy every minute of it.'

'Then let it start well. Carry me out to the stables, I have something to show you. Come along, David. And you too, Celina.'

Nicholas's narrowed gaze rested thoughtfully on David MacNeill. Such familiarity in only a week! Celina hung back, he noticed, and Marianna gave an exclamation of annoyance.

'Make her come, Nicholas. She chose your birthday present, after all.'

'Did she, now. Then she must indeed accompany us.' His tone belied argument and Celina followed them, wishing she could run and hide herself somewhere before Marianna told him how it had come about.

'There.' She pointed proudly to the red-coated stallion prancing continuously around the paddock. He seemed never to be still for a moment. There was a restlessness about him which made Celina feel he wanted desperately to be free. They were soul-mates, for they both yearned for the same thing.

'I thought you knew little of horses?' Nicholas looked at Celina in surprise. 'He is a magnificent animal. My thanks, Celina, this is a perfect choice.'

'She said he reminded her of you because he has wicked eyes,' Marianna giggled, and Celina felt her cheeks glow with embarrassed colour as Nicholas's gaze centred on her. His lips twitched as if he was holding back a smile, and those blue eyes, at that moment, had the devil's own laughter rising in them to taunt her.

'But then you know how to rouse the devil in me, don't you, Celina?' he returned softly.

CHAPTER
EIGHT

THE GUESTS began to arrive. Carriage-load after carriage-load for the next four hours. Servants met them on the steps and whisked away their luggage. Nicholas and Marianna welcomed them in the hall and Celina and Sulai showed them quickly upstairs to tidy up before bringing them back for the coffee and sweetmeats and cakes arranged in the respective rooms. The house buzzed with so much conversation it sounded like a drone of bees. Celina had never seen so much activity, or seen Marianna so happy. Or Nicholas so content as he stood by his sister's side and welcomed friends whom Celina knew he had not seen for many months, some for as long as a year.

Nicholas insisted on first taking his men friends to the stables to show them his newest acquisition. Celina heard great laughter come from the crowd as they walked away from the house. Was he telling them who had chosen it, and why? Jean appeared elegantly clad, wigged and powdered, and proceeded to play the attentive husband, deliberately elbowing David into the background. Unable to protest before so many eyes, Marianna was forced to accede to his wishes to push her chair or to carry her when the occasion arose. Celina had never seen him so attentive or so perfectly mannered and charming.

'Your penniless Scotsman has monopolised you enough of late, my love,' Celina heard him whisper once, when Marianna protested at David's absence from her side. 'You will have to put up with me today.' It was the nearest thing to a threat Celina had ever heard, and poor Marianna looked near to tears at the prospect of being accompanied by her husband throughout the day.

She did manage to escape briefly, closeting herself with all the other women in the sitting-room. Gossip flowed like water and Marianna was as interested to hear what was going on outside Paraíso as everyone else. Celina was introduced as her companion, without further explanations of how she came to be in Jamaica and she neatly side-stepped any prying questions until Jean gave away her past during lunch, as he sprawled beneath a shady tree, a glass of wine on the grass beside him and his arms folded behind his head. He was fast growing bored with being polite and dancing attendance on a useless wife. He had already made assignations with two pretty young daughters of a Kingston banker, and was eager to seize an opportunity to slip away. Nicholas stood talking to his nearest neighbour, between him and his objective, and Jean was furious to see the girls engaged in conversation with other men. Unable to take out his spite on Marianna, it fell on the first available person, who happened to be Celina.

Marianna had been inundated with invitations to visit friends in Kingston and Spanish Town, and Celina had been included too. She was thrilled at the prospect. Her short but satisfying spell in charge of the house had given her fresh confidence to meet people again, and the wardrobe which Nicholas had brought back with him would enable her to fulfil any engagement.

Instead of the plain dresses she had ordered, there

were bright colours and designs to suit every occasion. Satins, silks, brocades, velvets. She had never owned such clothes. The pride of her new wardrobe was the ball-gown made up from the bolt of white brocade threaded with silver, that Sulai had purchased for her. It was a stunning creation and she intended to wear it that evening. Paraíso was fast replacing the home she had lost, and she no longer felt guilty about it.

'You must come and stay with us, my dear.' A woman with three daughters of Celina's age was insisting that Marianna came to them for Christmas. Their plantation was on the opposite coast. 'And bring your companion with you. Such a charming young woman, so refined. How lucky you were to find such a treasure.'

'For that my wife cannot take the credit,' Jean murmured, eyeing the woman with malicious amusement. 'Nicholas's keen eye caught sight of Celina first. Quite a bargain, I believe. Only ten pounds.'

A startled gasp went through the onlookers. Celina's cheeks blenched. She wanted to strike out at his smiling face as tears blinded her vision. A hand fastened firmly over her arm.

'David, please take me back to the house,' she whispered miserably, as she turned away from the suddenly hostile faces regarding her and found herself looking up into Nicholas's blue eyes.

'You are not going to hide yourself away because my brother-in-law has the manners of a gutter-rat.' There was controlled anger in his voice, which quite clearly carried beyond her to those still listening with avid interest. 'Besides, I have not yet had the time to thank you for my present. Marianna, MacNeill has some food for you in the shade by the stream. I'll take you there. Ladies, if you will excuse me? I am sure Jean will be only to pleased to satisfy your curiosity about the details of Celina's background, and what he does not know he will make up. He has a talent for fantasy, that he applies to his own life, as well as to everyone else's.'

Celina could not refuse to accompany him, for he held fast to her wrist as he wheeled Marianna's chair away to where David had set up a small collapsible table beside the water. Xavier and Sulai were unpacking the last of the baskets and hampers. Children played on the grass around them and the atmosphere was carefree, except for the tiny area they had just left, Celina thought, as she looked back over her shoulder and saw heads huddled together. By the evening, her background would be known to everyone. The party was spoiled for her. She would not go.

'I know what you are thinking,' Nicholas said quietly. 'You will. You owe it to yourself. He cannot hurt you, Celina. Only you can do that.'

And you, she thought as he released her.

'You were wonderful, Nicholas. He becomes more offensive every day.' Marianna glared across the space between them, and then, realising how she had aroused her brother's interest, quickly said, 'He is always irritable at cutting-time, you know that. All the extra work . . .' It was a lame excuse and they all knew it. Soon, Nicholas thought, she would have to talk to him.

'How much food did you have prepared?' he asked, looking at the continuous flow of servants moving among the guests with large platters of cold ham and chicken-legs covered in breadcrumbs and plates of rolls which were replenished as quickly as they were depleted. There was wine in abundance, too, chilled with ice and deposited along the bank of the stream to keep it cool. And lime juice for the children, who seemed to have a never-ending thirst.

'I tried to ensure we would run out of nothing,' Marianna returned. 'I forgot to cater for one thing. Patience. I apologise for my husband, Celina. His rudeness was unforgivable.'

'He spoke the truth. I am what I am—a servant. Your friends are not as generous as you are. In their eyes I should keep to my place.'

'Without your help, none of this would have been possible,' Marianna insisted, her face concerned at the answer. 'I shall go nowhere without you, and I shall tell them that.'

'Now I hear my sister talking,' Nicholas drawled, biting into a chicken-leg with enthusiasm. 'By the way, where did you get those bruises?'

'Bruises! Oh, these.' Marianna quickly flicked the lace back over her wrists, angry not to have noticed that they were exposed to his gaze. In desperation, her eyes flew to David.

'My fault, I'm afraid. Your sister will insist on being too enthusiastic with the exercises I suggested she try in order to strengthen her leg muscles. I had her seated on the edge of the bed and she overbalanced. I grabbed her, without realising how fiercely. I have apologised, Captain Benedict. It will not happen again.'

Liar, Nicholas thought, as he nodded and looked away. Celina did not believe him either. He had seen the careful way the man touched his sister. Seen the way a simple gesture like handing her a book or a glass became almost a caress as their fingers touched. He had not anticipated a liaison between them, and it both worried and puzzled him. Was that the reason for her sudden differences of opinion with Jean? The estrangement between them? Was David MacNeill, along with her husband, competing for her favours? Celina would know, but would she tell him? he wondered. He stared into the thoughtful features a few feet away from him? Such petty remarks should not have hurt her, but they had. She was still vulnerable, and those gossiping hens would take advantage of it, given the chance. He *would* give them something to gossip about.

'Will you walk with me, Celina?' He rose to his feet, brushing stray leaves from his sleeves. Celina stared at the hand held out towards her. Heard Marianna quietly urge her to take it, and did so, knowing she wanted to be alone with David. It was madness to provoke further talk, but Celina suddenly did not care. His fingers were cool and firm on hers as he helped her to her feet and guided her away from the scattered groups of people. Curious eyes followed them; men winked knowingly at Nicholas, envying him his good luck, and went back to the important matter of eating and drinking. 'That should set the tongues wagging. By tonight they will have found someone else to tear to pieces. I'd forgotten what odious creatures some of them were.'

'Please don't tell Marianna that, or you will spoil the day for her. She thinks you are pleased with it.'

'And so I am. I can't remember when I've enjoyed a day more. You will come down tonight, won't you?'

'Is that a request or a command, sir?' Celina asked, gently, but determinedly pulling free her hand as soon as they were out of sight of everyone.

'Must I demand your presence? Can you not try and enjoy yourself on this special day?' Nicholas asked, glancing at her down-bent head. There were times, such as now, when her black hair had a blue sheen to it. She wore it loose about her shoulders, a marked contrast of colour against the whiteness of her skin.

'Is that one of the dresses I brought back?' he asked, admiring the way the saffron silk curved over firm breasts to a waist so slender that he wondered if it could be spanned by his two hands. She was still too thin, in his estimation.

'Yes. I have to thank you for changing my choices. They were very dull, but I thought . . .'

'Wear the white tonight,' Nicholas interrupted. 'And ask Marianna to lend you her pearls. Is she happy now, Celina? There was a time when you said she was not.'

'Yes, I think so.' She would be happier if Jean did not overshadow her life, she thought silently. As the mysterious Joanna overshadowed hers.

'Her association with your brother . . . MacNeill realises nothing can come of it.'

'Are you asking—or telling—me?' Celina looked into his face questioningly. 'If he has feelings other than friendship, admiration, respect for her, then I do not know of them. That is the truth.'

'I've seen the way he looks at her. Touches her,' Nicholas retorted with a frown. 'She might misinterpret . . .'

'Have you ever considered that she finds him attractive? Kind? Gentle? All the things her husband is not?'

'Go on,' he urged quietly.

'No, I have said too much already. It is not my place to talk of such things.'

'I am asking you to tell me. I know you have her interests at heart. For the past year she and Jean have not exchanged a harsh word in my presence. Now they do not care who hears them bickering, and those marks! I am not a fool. It was Jean, wasn't it?'

'Yes.' Celina knew it was useless to lie to him. They came to a grassy knoll where wild hibiscus bloomed in profusion. A fallen flower lay near the water. Nicholas bent and picked it up and offered it to her with a smile.

'A small token of my gratitude for all you have done for my sister. Now let us sit down—we shall not be disturbed here—and see if between us we cannot do more.'

His fingers brushed hers as she took the scarlet-petalled flower and slipped it into the neckline of her dress. Celina felt the colour mount in her cheeks as she spread her skirts about her and sat down. He reclined within touching distance, on one elbow, waiting for her to elaborate on what she felt.

'I think Jean feels—feels threatened by Marianna's sudden independence. While she was confined to bed he was free to come and go as he pleased, associate with whom he wished. This is very difficult for me . . .'

'Why? He is a womaniser, and we both know it. He has been after you for his bed since you arrived, hasn't he?' Nicholas demanded. 'I was a fool to bring him here, but I thought it was what she wanted. She loved him. She would die without him, she told me before they eloped. I thought then, and I still do, that she does not know the meaning of love, but after the accident . . . I felt responsible . . . I had to make amends . . .'

'How could you be held responsible for a runaway carriage?' Celina asked in puzzlement.

'When I found her gone from the house, I chased her all the way to Kingston, but it was too late. They had been married two hours before I arrived. Someone must have told her I was looking for her . . . she panicked, and ran again . . . Even while Jean and I were at each other's throats, she left the inn without a word . . .' Pain flooded into Nicholas's eyes, so much so that he could not hide it, and Celina's heart went out to him. 'Half a mile down the road something frightened the horses and they bolted. We found the carriage overturned, Marianna unconscious. You know the rest. I brought her back to Paraíso. Until you came, she had not left her bed.'

'And Jean? If you thought so little of him and did not want him as her husband, why is he here?'

He threw her a bitter look. A thousand times he had reproached himself for the mad act. He had brought her no happiness. A stranger had done that. No—two.

'Whatever I thought of him, she professed to love him. I had almost killed her with my damned obstinacy, my brotherly love that always knew what was best for her. She wanted Jean, and I gave him to her. When he knew she was crippled, he would have left, but I gave him no chance. I made him overseer, made it worth his while to remain and be with her, because I thought it was what she wanted. Now, I am no longer sure. You think that, if she walks again, Jean will leave her? Perhaps it's the best thing.'

'I don't know. I have the strangest feeling she might ask him to go,' Celina answered.

'And put your brother in his place? She'll not make another mistake,' Nicholas snapped harshly, and then laughed without humour. 'No. I will not run her life for her. If she makes mistakes, she will hear no reproach from me, nor shall I offer her advice. There is more of Father in her than she realises, though she would not like to hear me say it. "If you want something that will make you happy, take it," he always said. "Love is an elusive flame that dies as rapidly as it has been kindled. Or remains a deep burning ember which can flare to life again at any time and rule your life. Don't ignore it when it happens. Accept it, enjoy it and don't regret a single moment of anything that happens to you. It is all part of life's experience. Use it well." Poor Marianna. Her experience has not been a happy one.'

And yours, too, brought only sorrow, if she was to believe the rumours which linked him to his stepmother. For them both the flame of love had been kindled, yet was not strong enough to be sustained, and had died.

'Did—did he live by his own beliefs?' Celina asked hesitantly, and he gave a brief nod.

'He saw my mother, wanted her and married her. Built the house on the cliff for her. They were very happy. When she died, he was lost. Life held nothing for him. The plantation meant nothing without her here. He was so desperate to rekindle that flame that he married again. A girl young enough to be his daughter. My sister! It lasted a little over two years before her death released him.'

Had he helped that release come about, Celina wondered staring into the bronzed features.

'What are you thinking?' Nicholas demanded, aware of the violet eyes widening as she recalled the terrible scene Marianna had told her about.

'We—we should be returning to the others,' she said lamely. 'They will be wondering where we are. It is not right for you to neglect your guests.'

'On my birthday I shall do as I please, and it pleases me to be with you,' Nicholas replied, sitting up. 'Are you still happy, Celina? Could you be happier?'

'Yes. If I had my freedom,' she replied without hesitation, and he smiled at the answer as though he had been expecting it.

'That is but a small thing. Have you no dreams? Is there nothing you long for?'

'I have more than someone in my position usually has,' she said. Why was he asking such questions? The air of intimacy which had sprung unbidden between them, as on another occasion, made her uneasy. Nervous, like a girl at her first ball when a handsome man singled her out from all the others and gave her his attention. Why was she deserving of Nicholas's attention now?

'Damn your position. Are you not like all other women, desirous of jewels, fine clothes, a carriage and horses? You could have them all, you know.'

Celina drew back from him a look of horror on her face, interpreting his words to mean only one thing.

'You did not mean it,' she exclaimed. 'You said you would forget what was said between us. You never intended to, did you? You intend to hold me to our bargain?' Thinking of marriage, yet still he sought to seduce her!

'Bargain?' Nicholas's brows wrinkled into an annoyed frown. 'Oh, that! Why should I bargain for something already within my reach, Celina? All I have to do is reach out and take it! As you do! Come now, am I such a bad catch?'

'Do you not already have an accommodating mistress, sir? Are you not satisfied with her?' Celina's voice trembled. He had caught hold of her hand and drawn her towards him. She felt like a helpless fly waiting for the spider to devour her. If he touched her, she would betray herself. How many times had she recalled the strength of those arms, the wildness of his kisses, to make the ache in her heart intensify with longing.

'You little fool!' His voice was suddenly hard, the blue eyes blazing with something she could only think was anger at her insolence. For all his fine words he still thought of himself as her master, and expected her respect, not rudeness. 'You don't even realise what you are being offered,' he snapped, his mood changing without warning.

'I am not interested in becoming your mistress, or that of any other man.' Celina flung back her head and stared up into his face. How his touch weakened her. She had to fight against the pleasure it brought, the desire to surrender to his demands, and those of her own unrequited love. What did it matter if he did not care for her? This was the man she would love all her life. There would never be another. To spend a short while with him, to know a little happiness . . .

'Celina.' Her name was lost on his lips as he crushed her against him. His kisses had the expertise of a man who had known many women, she thought in panic. They were meant to bring her quickly to surrender. He pressed her back on the ground, his body holding hers fast beneath him. Celina knew he was too strong to be thrown off, knew she had to do something quickly before she lost all reason.

'Let me go!' She tore her mouth free from his, angry tears in her eyes. 'If you do not, I shall scream and bring help. You would not want people to see you tumbling one of your servants, would you, Captain Benedict?'

'Many of them had that in mind when they saw us leave,' Nicholas replied with a sardonic chuckle. 'Be still and listen to me, you infuriating wench.'

'I shall not!' she declared. She dared not! 'It was naive of me not to realise that you are no different from all the other men who have wanted me—merely more devious.' Her tone grew cold and accusing. 'Whom are you seeking to replace with me? Your mistress in Kingston? Or the woman you stole from your father?'

She cried out as his open palm struck her across one cheek. He drew back from her, and his face was terrible to see. Such fury . . . such condemnation and contempt

blazed out of it. She did not move as he stood up; she
could not. What had possessed her to hurl such wounding words at him? She had no proof. Yet was she not
seeing it now, in the way he looked at her? Proof that
forbidden love was far from dead? His mouth curled into
a twisted smile as he watched the marks of his fingers
slowly redden across her skin. He offered no words of
apology, only recrimination.

'Naive indeed!' he scathed, 'Naive of me, too, to
forget what treacherous bitches all women are! Get up,
girl, and go back to Marianna. It would not be wise to
anger me this way again,' he added, as she scrambled to
her feet. Her hair had come free of the combs confining
it and she desperately tried to gather it together in some
kind of order, dreading the eyes which would be on her
when she reappeared. Nicholas seized her by the wrists
as she fumbled with the long tresses, and shook her
roughly, his hard, brilliant eyes searching her face. 'Is
that what you think of me? You believe I loved her?'

'Yes. Yes!' she cried, sagging in his grasp. What else
was she to believe, given such a display of emotion?

'Damn you then!' he swore, and thrust her away from
him. 'You are not worthy of an explanation. Believe
what you will. Only you will lose by it.'

She turned and ran from him, picking up her skirts so
that they should not hamper her flight. He had loved
Soledad! The rumours were true, or he would have
denied them!

'Hurry and get ready,' Marianna insisted, as Celina
lingered in her room, watching the maid put the finishing
touches to her hair. Tonight it was curled and powdered
and adorned with brilliant ostrich-feathers to match the
exquisite green of her gown. Marianna had never looked

more beautiful or been so sure of what she wanted. Her freedom! An end to her marriage with Jean Leclerc. He had looked stunned when she had told him, then had laughed in her face and replied that he would leave when it suited *him*, not on the whim of a half-woman!

How that had cut her. He knew her eyes had been straying elsewhere, he told her in a threatening tone, and it would cease after tonight. After the ball, he would come to her, so that in the future she need not seek satisfaction with a penniless Scots rebel. It was then that Marianna decided to tell Nicholas the truth. It was the only way. Without his help she would be forced to endure the attentions of a man she had grown to loathe and fear. Not a trace of her distress showed on her face, however, as she considered Celina through the mirror of the dressing table where she sat.

'Did you hear me? It is time to go downstairs, and you are not even dressed.'

'Would you be displeased if I did not come down?' Celina asked in a quiet tone. 'I think I have been subjected to too much excitement. My head is throbbing fit to burst. Perhaps later, if I feel better . . .'

'Nonsense. You have allowed yourself to be upset by Lady Grayson's horrid remarks. Please, Celina, I want you too to enjoy yourself tonight. Nicholas,' she turned, appealing to the tall figure who appeared in the mirror behind her, 'Celina is pleading a headache to stay away from your party. You must not allow it. I think she fears more unpleasant gossip.'

Celina stood her ground as he turned and looked across at her. Like his sister, he had dressed for the occasion. She had never seen him so formally attired. His coat was of sapphire-blue brocade, heavily embroidered with gold thread. An abundance of white lace flowed from beneath the wide cuffs. More tumbled over the top buttons of the matching waistcoat. His breeches were a plain blue, his shoes black leather with large silver buckles. He wore his hair naturally, tied back with ribbon.

'Fear can make cowards of us all,' Nicholas replied with a faint shrug. 'Let her do as she pleases. Are you ready? Let me look at you.' He ignored her and inspected Marianna with admiration. 'I am so proud of you. Put your arms around my neck and I will carry you down. I have had the chair placed near the windows. It is an oppressive night and the room will soon grow stuffy with all the people in it. I think it will rain before the night is out.'

'Nicholas,' Marianna protested, staring over his shoulder to where Celina stood ashen-faced at his insult. He thought her a coward. She was, but her reasons were not those that Marianna was thinking.

'Our guests are waiting.' She heard Marianna still protesting as he carried her along the corridor, turned away in a miserable silence and began to tidy the room. Heard the sound of footsteps outside the door, and looked up to find Nicholas standing here. 'I have changed my mind. Go and get dressed. Why should you escape so lightly?'

'Please let me stay up here? It matters not to you!' She was aghast at the order. Was this the punishment he had devised for her words that afternoon? He knew she would not, could not, enjoy herself now.

'Whether it does or not is not your concern. You will do as you are told. You are always so quick to remind me of your position in this house. Now I am reminding you. I am master here, and you shall obey me.'

Wordlessly, she went to her own room, with him

following close on her heels. He waited in the sitting-room while her maid helped her to dress. When she reappeared he turned from the window and stared at her, and said stiffly, 'Turn round and let me look at you.'

Again she obeyed without a word. What else could she do? The white brocade had been adorned with four rows of Brussels lace round the skirt and sleeves, and small bows on the bodice. The open skirt revealed an under-skirt of silver flounced brocade. She had refused the addition of the large panniers which were coming back in to fashion, preferring the beautiful gown to fall naturally about her hips. The black hair was caught up in a mass of curls at the back of her head, and held there by combs set with pearls. She had no jewellery to wear, save the locket the 'Fox' had given her, and she had not asked Marianna for her pearl necklace, as she had had no intention of showing herself that evening.

Nicholas realised it, too, as he stared at the smooth expanse of white shoulders, the smooth rise of her breasts above a neat little lace bow. She was lovely beyond all description, and he would not relinquish his claim to her no matter what she thought of him. She would have to live with her suspicions, as he must with his, if he was to keep her with him.

'Why?' The question broke from trembling lips.

'Because it pleases me, Celina. You will learn in time to do as I wish without question,' came the softly veiled warning.

'And if I do not, you will no doubt send my brother back to the fields.'

'No. What is between us will be settled without in-volving anyone else. One more thing,' he added, as she moved like a sleep-walker towards the door. 'There will be no more afternoon walks to the old house.

Do I make myself clear?'

She wheeled about, lips parting in a gasp of horror. How had he known? Jean? He nodded, confirming her unasked question. His eyes burned mercilessly into her face.

'And you have the audacity to sit in judgment on my actions?' He gave a humourless smile. 'We are well matched, it seems. Mistrust comes easily to us both.'

'Will you excuse me a moment, I have forgotten something.' Her features set in a determined manner, Celina went back to her bedroom. When she re-emerged, the locket the 'Fox' had given her was about her throat. She met Nicholas's gaze challengingly. It had been given in friendship; she cared no more what he thought.

'Where did you get that?' There was surprise in his tone, but no anger, and it unbalanced her. She had been prepared for the most scathing of comments.

'Jean did not know whom I went to meet. It was your friend, the "Fox". When I realised someone was using the house I went to tell them to leave, but he told me it was with your permission.'

'He needs none to be there,' Nicholas said, so low it could almost have been to himself.

'I have been there several times. I liked him and I—I liked his company. Think what you will about that, Captain Benedict. You cannot malign me any more than you have. He gave me this locket and I took it because . . . because he was a lonely old man, grateful for a few hours of my company, and this was his way of thanking me.'

'A lonely old man,' he repeated, brows furrowed. 'Yes, he is that. I'd forgotten how lonely. So you thought he was grateful for your company. My God, girl, you don't know him like I do. So he thinks to turn your head with pretty trinkets, does he? Well, he'll lose this one. You are mine.'

With those chilling words he took Celina's arms and propelled her to the head of the stairs. Her mind reeled at his words, then slowly, as she became aware of the heads turning to watch them descend, she was filled with pity for the man at her side who saw no good in anyone. Turn her head! He could not have been more mistaken. Only one man could do that, and he would be for ever unaware of it.

Jean's jaw dropped visibly as he danced past them, a giggling young girl in his arms. Nicholas guided her through the throng of people to where Marianna sat, David at her side. He belonged there, Celina thought, and she prayed that, although her life seemed destined to take a disastrous road, he would find happiness with the woman of his choice.

'Celina, I am so glad Nicholas persuaded you, after all. Come and sit with me for a while, 'Marianna said smilingly.

David gasped in admiration, and kissed his sister. There was a question in his eyes, she saw, as they fell to the fingers still gripping her arm. Had she been persuaded, or forced? The relationship puzzled him, and she could not explain without arousing bitterness between the two men who were now friends. Whatever Nicholas thought of her, he had not backed out of his agreement with her brother. He was a freed man with papers in his possession to prove it, and already, he had told her as they came back to the house after lunch, he had been approached by prospective patients. He would soon have a chance to use the instruments Nicholas had purchased for him in Kingston.

'Next year,' Nicholas said quietly, bending to kiss

Marianna on the cheek, 'I shall dance with my sister, the most attractive woman in the room tonight. Will you make me that promise?'

'Gladly.' Perhaps you will not want to dance or even speak to me when you hear what I have to say, Marianna thought, fighting to keep the smile on her face.

'I shall just have to be content with the second best until then.' His fingers tightened still more over Celina's arm, warning her against a refusal. 'I am sure Celina dances as competently as she does everything else. Shall we see?'

As the musicians struck up a tune, he led her into the midst of the dance-floor, to the envy of many of the men present and the jealousy of half the women.

'So you found the "Fox" a pleasant enough character, did you?' Nicholas murmured. 'For your information, he's little more than an out-and-out pirate and only his letters of marque from the Governor keep him from the scaffold. Even those won't save him one of these days.'

'Are you now prepared to belittle a friend because he was kind to me instead of attempting seduction?' Celina asked in a low tone, conscious of the faces watching them. 'I find that attitude beneath contempt.'

'There is much about me you do not like of late.'

'Like,' she echoed, eyes frosty as they stared up into the smiling features. 'How can I like a man who owns me? No more can I respect him.'

'Tread carefully. You will not be safe from my anger because these people are about us!' There was a danger-ous edge to his voice she had learned to recognise. It was time to hold her tongue.

It was a relief when he returned her to Marianna's side and left to partner someone else. Celina had never thought herself capable of jealousy until she watched him with an attractive young girl, who spent every minute with him, fluttering her eyelashes and peering at him coyly from behind a huge ivory fan.

If anyone spoke to Marianna, Celina was mostly ignored, and, as the evening wore on, the continual snubs began to wear on her nerves. David took her hand with a smile, sensing the tumult building inside her.

'Am I allowed one dance with my sister?'

'Thank you,' Celina breathed as they merged with the others on the floor. Beside him and him alone could she relax for a while. 'I feel as if I am slowly and systematically being torn to shreds by some of these gossiping hens.'

'It won't last. The captain has made it quite clear that he considers you almost part of the family. I thought it was a nice gesture to dance first with you.'

'Gesture,' she murmured bitterly. 'He is good at those. Oh, Davie, I wish I had never come to this place. Not that I had any choice.'

'I thought you were happy here. It is the impression you have given me, even though this relationship with Captain Benedict worries me from time to time. From one day to the next I never know how the two of you are going to react when you come together,' David said, searching her face for answers and finding none. She was so adept at hiding her feelings from him. Once it would have been impossible.

'The colourful reputation I acquired on board the prison ship will for ever be with me,' his sister whispered miserably. 'The captain watches my every move, suspects an ulterior motive if I so much as speak to another man. And Jean's attentions to me have not helped matters. Even though the captain knows the kind of man he is, he still believes I would welcome Jean's advances.'

'Then he cares for you?' David said in surprise.

'On the contrary. I am a piece of property which belongs to him and which he intends to ensure belongs to no other man. Oh, I wish I did not love him so.' She broke off with a gasp. 'Davie, never repeat that to anyone, even Marianna. Promise me?'

'If it is that you wish. My poor lass, I am no help to you, am I? Fortune smiles on me and turns its back on you. If I spoke to him . . .'

'No. It is something I must work out for myself. Take me back, Davie. I feel a thousand eyes boring into my back.'

As they approached Marianna's chair, they saw Jean move away into the crowd around the buffet table, leaving his wife ashen-faced and trembling.

'What is it? What did he say?' David demanded, taking one of her hands in his, not caring who saw him or what comments were passed. The time was fast approaching when he knew he must disclose his intense feelings for this girl at his side, offer her more than comfort, more than sympathy and guidance, little though it was.

'David, I am so afraid. The things he said . . . When I am really his wife, he is going to have you sent away . . . I don't know how, he didn't say, but you can imagine the rumours, the terrible stories he could spread about you. You would have no patients . . . I doubt if even Nicholas could stop the gossip which would spread. Jean is hinting already that Celina is not your sister . . . that in Scotland . . .' She gave a soft cry and hid her face behind her fan. 'Where is Nicholas? I must talk to him.'

'Across the far side of the room with at least a dozen people. It must wait, Marianna, until later. I will stay with you for the rest of the evening.'

'But when I go upstairs . . .' she said fearfully.

'Celina or I will be with you and we shall remain with you until your brother comes. Don't fret, love. Jean will not touch you again, I swear it,' David said in a harsh whisper. Before a dozen pairs of curious eyes, he touched her fingers to his lips. 'Let them ogle us. Their gossip cannot harm us.'

How brave he was. How sure of himself, Celina thought, as she left them, intent on each other. Jean would not harm Marianna while her brother stood near. She was hungry, but there was a mass of people about the tables spread with the food, and she had no wish to display herself for more comment. She turned towards the open french windows and the solitude of the gardens. The full moon was almost obscured by heavy cloud. It would rain before morning, she thought, but at least it had held off for today. It was a day she would remember for many reasons. She had not lied when she told Marianna her head ached. It had not stopped all evening.

Beneath a leafy arbour she sat down and closed her eyes, only to open them with a start, as a voice declared close by, 'And what is the prettiest girl at the party doing sitting alone?'

The 'Fox' stood on the path in front of her. And the transformation from the man she had seen at the old house was startling. Like most of the guests, he was wigged and elegantly dressed. A gentleman!

'You did invite me,' he chuckled, as Celina came to her feet, unable to believe her eyes. He had come, after all, although he thought Nicholas would not be pleased to see him. 'What are you doing out here, pretty lass? Are there no men inside to dance with? Give me your arm, then, and come and dance with me. Afraid of the old maids inside? Or Nicholas, perhaps,' he chided, when she did not accept the offered arm.

'He knows I came to see you. He thought it quite amusing.'

'Did he, now? Then let's wipe the smile from his face and go in together.'

Why not, Celina thought. She could not be talked about more. She took his arm and allowed him to lead her back into the noisy room. He commanded two glasses of champagne. As Celina sipped the ice-cold bubbling contents of her glass, the man beside her chuckled softly.

'Have you ever seen so many gaping mouths, my dear? Don't they remind you of fishes out of water?'

She had to smile at the comparison. Heads were turned in their direction, faces expressing surprise if not amazement at the couple who stood on the edge of the throng. The 'Fox' was known to many of them, Celina thought in puzzlement, but how? Several men even nodded in his direction. The women turned their backs and whispered behind gloved hands. *They* did not approve of him.

'And here comes Nicholas to welcome me to his party.'

He came threading his way through the dancers, his eyes intent on the 'Fox'. More heads turned to watch his progress. Why did she think they were all waiting for some kind of confrontation, she wondered? At the far end of the room she could see Marianna sitting bolt upright in her chair, a hand against her mouth.

'I did not expect to see you here tonight.' Nicholas halted in front of them both. She could read nothing from his expression, and the eyes which glanced briefly at her were cold and guarded. 'How are you, Father?'

Father! Had he said 'Father'? The 'Fox' was John Benedict!

CHAPTER
NINE

'THIS IS the man you have been meeting?' As her mind reeled with unanswered questions, Nicholas looked at Celina, ignoring the smile on the face of his father as he finished his champagne and promptly helped himself to another, as a full tray was carried past.

'Yes.'

'Why did you not tell me when I came back? Why was it necessary to hear it from Jean? You must realise the pleasure he took in telling me you had been secretly meeting someone while I was away?'

'And what would you have thought?' Celina stared at him, her tone defiant. 'You have made it clear I can do nothing without your approval. Would you believe we had merely talked?'

'My father is not exactly senile,' came the dry retort, and she blushed furiously. 'I have inherited the Benedict trait of mistrust. I admit I was hasty in my judgment.'

'As in all others you have made of me,' she flung back disdainfully. 'Between you and Jean my reputation has grown even more colourful since I came to Paraíso. Half the people here think I am your mistress, the others believe I am David's. Jean has been telling them we are not brother and sister.'

'The devil he has,' Nicholas ejaculated. 'He'll answer to me for any trouble he causes. You look well, Father.

Have you come for my birthday, or do your interests in being here tonight lie in another direction?' He was still looking directly at Celina as he spoke. 'Is history about to repeat itself?'

'Don't use that insolent tone with me, you young fool!' the 'Fox' retorted. 'I learned my lesson. It appears that you have not. Not all women are scheming bitches like she was. This child is lonely and unhappy, mostly due to you, from what I hear. Afraid of you, she is. Now there's a fine thing. Gentleness, that's what she wants. Have you none to give her?'

'You have, it seems,' Nicholas returned stiffly, and John Benedict laughed.

'I'm too old to play games any more, and I no longer search for the impossible. I am content with my memories.'

'Then we understand each other. Celina is mine.'

'If you can hold her. She said you were unpredictable, lad. Perhaps you've changed, but I see no sign of it. How long has it been this time . . . a year?'

'Fourteen months,' Nicholas interrupted, and Celina knew that the outward show of antagonism was but a façade. He had missed his father—had counted the months.

'Too long for a father and son to be apart. A father and daughter also.' John Benedict's eyes travelled to the end of the room where Marianna sat. 'Will she speak to me?'

'I don't know. Are you prepared to speak to her?' Nicholas asked quietly. 'Don't you think you have ignored her existence long enough? She's fast growing up, Father. God willing, in a few months—less, maybe, with MacNeill's help, she will walk again.'

'MacNeill? Celina's brother. I've heard much of him.

This pretty lass was as hungry for conversation as I was. I know all about your proposition to him. The MacNeills of Craig Tor have become like a second family to me these past few days,' he said with a smile, and Celina quickly averted her gaze as Nicholas stared at her intently.

She had talked to his father, and willingly, it seemed, but for the son she had neither time nor conversation until he forced her. The anger which had been seething inside him since Jean had poisoned his mind that afternoon was fast receding. It had both amused and concerned him to discover his own father was the man she had been meeting, but looking now at them both, he knew there was nothing between them except a strange bond of friendship that had developed quickly and surely and would not be broken. And yet he had failed to reach her.

How can I like a man who owns me? No more can I respect him? What if she were free? Would she flee Paraíso? To win, to have her prepared to stay willingly with him, he knew he must be prepared to lose her.

'You are making Marianna more uncomfortable by not approaching her. Come, Father.' Celina laid her hand on the arm Nicholas offered. He could feel her trembling. Was she afraid of him? Of a few stolen kisses? Or did she fear herself and the knowledge that somewhere deep inside her was the response he sought when she was in his arms?

Marianna, still sitting rigidly in her chair, sought the comfort of David's hand as she watched the trio approach. The colour was gone from the cheek she turned away as John Benedict bent to kiss her.

'Father.' She acknowledged him with a frosty look. How dare he come here, tonight of all nights, and spoil her enjoyment? Between them, he and Jean were ruining the evening. The pressure of David's fingers curled tightly around hers gave her courage to remain withdrawn.

'Have you no kiss for your father?' he asked, stepping back, a hurt look on the weathered features.

'Should I have? Since when did you remember I was your daughter?' she demanded in a fierce whisper. People were watching them curiously. Jean had left his dancing partner and was heading in her direction. She glanced gratefully up at Celina as the other girl saw him and moved protectingly to the other side of the chair.

'I am well deserving of your anger and bitterness and your reproach,' John said, and Celina's heart went out to him. Whatever it was that had kept them apart for so long, John wanted an end to it. 'I admit I have been no father to you. My only excuse is that I loved too well; and when I lost your mother, and you were in her place, you were no substitute, my dear. One day, if you ever find a man to love as I loved her, then you will understand. There can be no replacement. I tried, with Soledad, and brought more misery to this house and to you and your brother. To myself. Is there no forgiveness in your heart for a tired, lonely old man who would like to come home and be with his family again? Or do I no longer have a family?'

Huge tears shone in Marianna's eyes. She did not want to be affected by his words—he had brought her too much unhappiness—but they touched her soul. He looked what he said he was, a tired, lonely old man. He had nothing without them, despite all his travels, his searching for a replacement for her beloved mother, and he had nowhere to go but Paraíso.

'Come . . . come home?' she stammered. 'Live here

with us again? So that you and Nicholas can be at each other's throats again over her—that Spanish woman?' She had never called her stepmother by name in the two years she had been married to John, never considered her to be anything but an outsider who would never belong at Paraíso.

'Nicholas and I have long since given up that foolish quarrel. In my jealousy I accused him of many things, the most unforgivable being the seducer of my wife. I should have known that my son protected, not destroyed, what was mine. He and Soledad were never involved in an affair, my child. You believed it to be so and many other people did, many of them in this room, listening to us with bated breath, but it was not.'

'The night she died . . . I saw her run out of the library. I saw the look on Nicholas's face when he went after her. An hour later she was dead,' Marianna said, still in a hushed tone. She had long forgotten there were other people about them. Her eyes did not leave her father's face. Celina's could not leave Nicholas's. No affair! He could have told her, yet he did not. He allowed her to think the worst of him, as he did of her!

'She was . . . *enceinte*.' John's features tightened with pain as he divulged the secret he and his son had kept between them for so long. 'Not *my* child. When I remonstrated with her that night, she laughed in my face and told me of her lovers . . . that she and Nicholas . . . I was beside myself with rage. I believed anything of her. Stupidly, of him too. You were right just now, Nicholas. We Benedicts have the trait of mistrust in our blood. It destroyed me, but it must not destroy you or Marianna. Do not let it rule either of your lives as it has mine these past years.'

'Soledad was mad with rage, too,' Nicholas said to his

sister. His eyes were for her, but his words were for
Celina. 'She told Father the child was mine, and he
believed her. Had I caught her, I think I would have
killed her for causing such ill-feeling between us. I had
ignored her attempts to take up with me, kept quiet
when I knew she was flirting with other men, until her
behaviour began to grow so outrageous that I warned
her, if she did not settle down and become the wife and
mother Father expected, I would tell him the truth and
have her thrown off Paraíso. To get back at me, she told
him I was the father of her child. I was not. I had never
touched her that way.'

Celina found she was tightly gripping the padded
arm of Marianna's chair. Not her lover! How they had
misjudged each other. If only he was as willing to
acknowledge his mistake as she was hers.

Marianna stretched out her arms, her eyes flooded
with tears.

'Welcome home, Father,' she said tremulously.

His face alight with joy, John Benedict went down on
one knee and embraced her. Celina was sure she had
glimpsed a tear in his eye, too, and she did not feel very
composed herself. Nicholas was looking straight at her,
reminding her of the shameful accusation she had flung
in his face earlier that day. Was he waiting for an
apology?

'Marianna, I think it is time I took you upstairs, *ma
petite*.'

Jean stood beside Celina. He stared with a haughty
expression at the man who rose to his feet. How many
men did his wife feel it necessary to have around her?
She was attracting them like flies. He would have to
remind her whom she belonged to, so that this show of
independence did not continue.

'You have not met my father, have you, Jean?' Nicholas said, smouldering resentment in his eyes at the unwarranted intrusion. 'John Benedict, Marianna's husband, Jean Leclerc.'

'I've heard of you, too,' John said in a sour tone, as Jean sketched a bow at the introduction. He had heard much, too, of the legendary 'Fox', privateer of great repute. He had often been forced to withstand sneers and backhanded insults because he was a Frenchman by birth and this man before him preyed on French ships and made a profitable living from it.

'I am delighted at last to meet my famous father-in-law,' he replied suavely. Until he had dealt with Marianna, his position was too precarious to do anything other than be polite to this accursed man.

'I think I prefer my daughter's second choice,' John said coldly, looking down at the slim fingers which had returned to seek comfort in David's hand.

'You are insulting, M'sieur,' Jean gasped.

'I am at your disposal any time you wish to do anything about it. As I said, I know about you too, Leclerc. As well as disliking you for being my daughter's husband, I dislike your choice of friends in Kingston and Spanish Town. You should tread carefully in my sight.'

'I have no idea what you are talking about.' Jean's face had lost some of its haughtiness. Was that a flicker of fear she saw pass through his eyes, Celina wondered? The two men had never met before, but the 'Fox' knew him—or knew of him.

'Your background and connections are well known to me. I happen to mix in the same low circles from time to time. We have mutual acquaintances on the waterfront.'

Jean looked uncomfortable. Either his visits to the French agent in Spanish Town were known, or his many sojourns at a disreputable house of pleasure. The disclosure could not have come at a worse time for him. He had to bluff his way out. Marianna was still his wife, his lever—his shield between himself and this new threat.

'Marianna, I shall take you upstairs, now, it is getting late,' he said, turning back to her.

'No.' She brushed aside the hands outstretched to lift her from the chair. 'I don't want to go up yet.' Her voice was tinged with a note of panic that brought a frown to Nicholas's features.

'I insist,' Jean replied softly. 'If MacNeill here was anything of a doctor and not the quack I know him to be, he would never have allowed you to exert yourself like this. As your husband, I must insist you obey me. I have your best interests at heart, *mignonne*, you know that. Come, let me carry you.'

'Don't touch her,' David snapped, and stepped in front of the chair.

'Stand aside, young man,' John Benedict ordered. 'It is not your place to come between them. Stand aside, or I shall have you removed.'

'Please, do as he says,' Marianna begged. 'Father, please listen . . .'

'No, you listen to me, my girl. You are husband and wife and this thing must be settled between you.'

'I salute your wise counsel,' Jean said and he began to smile, reaching once more for his wife as David stood back, slowly, reluctantly, with loathing on his face and a feeling of helplessness in his heart. He would not touch her! He had promised her and, no matter what he had to do to keep that promise, he would.

'Stand aside, Leclerc. You have no more right to her than he has,' John thundered, and people who had been drifting closer, curious to catch a snatch of conversation, warily moved away again, sensing more to this conflict than a mere casual dispute among family. He looked at his daughter, recognised the terrible fear in her heart, and assumed the responsibility of parenthood with a great surge of exaltation sweeping through him. At last he could do something to prove to her he was back to stay, to offer comfort and guidance as a father should; and love, if she would accept it. 'I don't know what is between you, only that you no longer wish to be his wife.'

'I have never been that. The accident prevented it . . .'

'Do you wish the marriage annulled? Judge Parker is here tonight, I noticed. I shall speak with him if you agree?'

Annulment! Freedom to be with David! Jean's eyes burned into her face. The threat mirrored there almost made her lose her fast failing courage. She could not speak. She nodded, and heard him swear beneath his breath.

'Then you must tell him so here and now. Openly. Give me your hand,' her father ordered.

'Sir, that's impossible,' David protested. He was going to make her stand and face Jean. He would ruin all his weeks of painstaking labour. Or would he? The determined expression which settled on Marianna's face held him silent, when every instinct he possessed cried out to stop this madness. She was not that strong. Not yet.

Marianna stared at the hand before her. Get up, get up, a voice screamed inside her. I cannot! I can! I shall fall. No! I will walk!

'This lady requires the assistance of two good hands, Father,' she said, smiling faintly. Now, before she

turned to jelly and burst into tears. Now! They would
not hold her! She could feel her legs beneath her . . .
The hands gripping hers were strong, so strong, urging
her on. Her legs were holding her! It felt as if a thousand
red hot pins were being thrust into them, but they were
supporting her. She was standing!

'Oh, well done, Marianna! Oh, look everyone!
Marianna can walk!' someone exclaimed, and a great
shout of admiration went up around her. Walk! Yes, she
could walk. She would. Poor David, he looked so worried, but she had to do it. For his sake as much as for
hers. If she did not, they would never be free to live the
life they had begun to plan in those hours closeted
together. Celina had a hand against her mouth, her eyes
wide with anticipation; and Nicholas, such pride blazed
out of his face. How lucky she was to have such friends—
such a family. From today her life would begin again and
she would show them how much she loved them all. All
of them in their own ways had made it possible for her to
do this. Her father! It would be strange to call him that,
but she would grow used to it and to having him in the
house again. The Benedicts were a family again,
reunited, never to be parted by suspicions or mistrust.

The hubbub of voices receded into the background;
she swayed unsteadily.

'Look what you are doing to her!' she heard Jean
exclaim. 'Give her to me at once. I demand you give me
my wife!'

Demand? His wife? Never! Not while she lived!

'I am not and never shall be your wife,' she said in a
loud, clear voice. 'There has never been anything between us and there never shall be. I want to be free of
him, Father. I want our marriage to end.'

'You heard her, Leclerc. Make this as unpleasant as

possible for as many of us as possible.' Scathingly, Nicholas stepped forward. Marianna had made her decision and she would have her wish. Her life was now in her own hands, and he thought her well able to manage it. He suspected that David MacNeill would quickly become a part of it, but there would be no questions, no voicing of his own opinions as before. She was her own mistress and would make her own mistakes. He did not think she would make many in his capable hands. The miracle he had prayed for had come about. She would walk! He took no credit for it, even though his purchase of Celina had been the starting-point, the instrument he had used to make his sister aware of herself again, conscious of how small her troubles were in relation to those of others, of how she could overcome them with new heart. Marianna had found that Celina and her brother and their father's return had sealed the final page in her struggle to succeed. 'I think it advisable for you and I to meet first thing in the morning to discuss your departure.'

'I'll see you in hell first!' Jean spun around on Nicholas, nostrils flaring and, as his eyes fastened on Celina standing at his side, his vindictiveness knew no bounds. 'You did this. You parted us. Ever since you came here, flaunting yourself in front of every man on Paraíso, Marianna has not been the same. You have poisoned her mind against me. You, who have the morals of an alley-cat! How many men did you favour before your present master, bitch? He's only using you, you realise that, don't you? He doesn't believe all that doe-eyed honesty any more than I did. We had some good times together while you were away, Benedict, but even I couldn't hold her. She found another to go to, as I told you.'

'Are you referring to Celina's visits to the old house?' John asked. Celina's face was drained of all colour. She dared not look at Nicholas, dreading what she might see in his eyes. Jean would be believed, of course. With her reputation she had no chance of redeeming her good name. 'She came to see me. Are you suggesting there was a liaison between us? I have done many things in my life, but I have no more stolen my son's woman than he did mine. You slimy son of a French toad, I think I shall kill you for those words.'

'No, Father, you will have to stand in line.' Nicholas's fingers seized the hand about to strike Jean across the face. 'You have until dawn to leave Paraíso, Leclerc. If I find you here then, I shall myself kill you. And there will be a dozen men here present tonight who will witness it. Xavier!' Jean wheeled with a sharp intake of breath to find the negro servant directly behind him. There was death in the black eyes which stared at him. 'See him to his room, assist him to pack his belongings, but do not lay one finger on him. Is that understood?'

'Yes, Captain.'

'You cannot let him go with Xavier,' Celina protested. 'Sulai is reason enough for him to kill Jean.'

'He will do nothing. I can trust him,' Nicholas assured her. 'You are concerned for him? You would like to go with him, perhaps? Leave Paraíso?'

He was offering to let her go? She could not believe her ears. His son's woman, John Benedict had called her. Not yet, but, if she remained, she would be. His mistress only, like the woman in Kingston. She would have fine things, jewels perhaps, and the carriage he had spoken of, but she would be an outcast among his friends, as much as she was now. She would have him and yet she would not, for she knew no woman had ever owned Nicholas Benedict. Perhaps there was not one alive who could. Her love would turn sour, become resentment, even hate. She would be used, tolerated, cast aside when he grew tired of her. She would never have his love!

'Yes, I wish to leave Paraíso. Alone, but there is no chance of that, is there, Captain Benedict?'

'I'll take her off your hands,' a bearded man chuckled to one side of them, only to be pushed aside by a woman in her late seventies, heavily powdered and rouged, her hands and arms covered in glittering jewels.

'Stand aside, Calvert. This poor girl is not going to be bartered off to any man. If you have no further use for her, Nicholas, I shall take her into my household. I have no young men to ogle her. I'm a cantankerous old woman who will demand all her time, but I'll provide well for her. Who knows, I may even find a suitable husband for her. What do you say? Will you let me have her?'

'Nicholas!' Marianna gave a cry of horror and collapsed into her father's arms, her eyes tightly closed.

'Your future, it seems, must be held in abeyance, but I think we are both in agreement, that the sooner you leave Paraíso, the better,' Nicholas said tersely. 'Take Marianna upstairs, Father. Go with them, MacNeill; she is going to need your medical skills. You too, Celina. Until you leave here you will be as useful as you can.'

As Celina mounted the stairs behind John Benedict and his unconscious burden, David's arm around her shoulders, she saw Nicholas pushing his way through the crowded room towards the door, his expression as black as thunderclouds. He was allowing her to leave! From one prison into another, she thought miserably, averting her gaze from the woman who wished to buy her from him. She would stifle in such an atmosphere after the existence at Paraíso. And she would never see him again! That was the price she must pay for loving him.

'Do you know what you are doing?' David bent his head low towards hers, so that his voice did not carry to the man in front of him. Sulai came running up behind them, her face portraying the concern she felt as she saw Marianna's limp form. She had been organising extra food in the kitchen when an excited maid brought the news of Jean's confrontation with Nicholas and his father. Tomorrow the only cloud overhanging her happiness would be lifted. And if she was any judge of character, which she prided herself she was, the young doctor would compensate Marianna for the loss of her husband. Yet instead of happiness, of jubilation, Marianna was in a faint; the old captain looked as if he would like to murder someone; Celina . . . never had Sulai seen her look so distraught, not even that day she had been brought aboard Nicholas's ship and she had wept in the woman's arms, thinking her life was not worth living. Over the past weeks Sulai had watched her begin to blossom like a young flower-bud in the sunshine. Had seen too, the way Nicholas watched her. Wanting her, she suspected, yet not daring to take what was his by rights. That puzzled her. The longing in him for this lovely Scottish girl was great indeed, Xavier had confirmed that. Begrudgingly, but he had confirmed it, and Sulai had smiled in that way of hers which greatly annoyed him, because he knew she had been right all along in her assumptions. Nicholas had bought the girl for himself.

Celina nodded, not wishing to answer him with Sulai listening intently only inches away from them. David frowned at her silence. She loved the man, yet she chose to leave him. Despite the liking which had grown be-tween them, he wished he had succeeded in beating Nicholas when he had had the chance and so attained some kind of guarantees for his sister's future. Instead, he had allowed himself to be swayed by her words which had been meant to dissuade him from further fighting and, he realised, save him from certain death. He had so much waiting for him in the future—she had nothing. What Cumberland's soldiers, months in prison and transportation had failed to achieve, Nicholas Benedict had.

'MacNeill, come here and see to your patient,' John ordered, laying Marianna down on the bed. 'Sulai, fetch some brandy and water. Celina, will you stay with her throughout the night? I don't trust our French friend.'

'Of course. I shall not leave her side,' she promised, and he patted her hand gratefully as he stepped back from the bed.

'With your permission, I too will remain,' David said. Marianna was in the throes of recovering consciousness. He did not know how she would react when she came to, and he wanted to be near her. 'I no more trust Leclerc than you do, and my sister, hellion though she is reputed to be, would be no match for him if he broke in here and gave her trouble.'

'Stay then. Guard her well. She is precious to me, as I think you both realise. I must speak with Nicholas.'

'He—he has left, I think.' Celina offered the infor-mation falteringly. John turned and stared at her, his mouth set in a tight line.

'The young fool has as much to learn as you have, Mistress. You will not leave Paraíso.' It was framed as a statement rather than a question.

'I must.'

'Then you are as big a fool as he is.' The man scowled at her, before the door closed behind him.

'I agree with him,' David said. Marianna stirred in the bed and he turned to give her his full attention. Sulai returned with brandy and water. She gave him a glass for Marianna and then brought one for Celina. She did not refuse. Sulai thought her mad too, Celina thought, as the woman went to the bed and laid a damp towel across the girl's forehead. Was she the only one who saw the necessity for such a drastic decision? Did they not realise that to become Nicholas's mistress, without love or genuine affection, would destroy her? Take from her the tremendous will to survive that had maintained her throughout all her troubles?

A clock somewhere in the house struck six times, rousing Celina from her slumber. David sat in a chair beside the bed where Marianna now slept fitfully under the influence of a heavy sleeping-draught. His eyes were closed, but she knew he was not asleep. As the sound of the door alerted her she quickly sat up, but relaxed again as Xavier came quietly into the room.

'I am to stay with her for a few hours until Sulai comes,' he said in a low tone. 'You and the doctor must rest now.'

'I will stay,' David said from his chair.

'There is no need. Leclerc has gone, hours ago, before the party ended. The captain gave me instructions to come and sit with the young mistress, and so I am here. A little late, I'm afraid. One of the guests wanted to leave very early this morning and I had to saddle his horse and see to his luggage on the way. Go and rest, both of you. Sulai will come soon.'

'He is right, Davie, we must sleep,' Celina said,

stifling a yawn. 'Marianna will not wake for hours and if Jean has gone she is in no danger. Where—where are Captain Benedict and his father, Xavier?'

'The captain rode off hours ago, just after you all came upstairs, and Captain John followed him a while later. I think they will be at the old house. Getting drunk, maybe?' The ebony face broke into a smile. To see the two men together had warmed his soul. It was as it had once been between them.

'I won't be able to sleep,' Celina said as she and her brother stood in the corridor, watching the sky lighten through one of the windows. 'Besides, I expect the captain will wish to be rid of me as soon as possible. I must go, Davie. You know why. Hold me a moment. Let me take a little of your strength with me. I shall have need of it.'

'You intend to go willingly with that old woman, then, if he lets you go?'

'Yes.'

'I can't let you go. It is not necessary. I shall speak to him, no matter what you say. You are throwing away a good life here,' David exclaimed in exasperation.

'Then I would run away,' Celina insisted. 'Words, Davie, that's all they would be. He has to trust me with his heart, and that is impossible for him to do. Sometimes I see the way he looks at me . . . when he has held me . . .' Her voice trailed off beneath her brother's startled gaze. 'I would be mistress of his bed, but not of his heart, and not long in his bed at that. That woman Joanna, that he sees in Kingston. He's more or less said they are to be married soon. Don't you see, I am a diversion until he can have what he really wants. A passing fancy until he can have her! Have I sunk to such a level, Davie? Is that what you want for me?'

'No, by God! No!'

'Then kiss me and let us walk for a few minutes in the gardens before you retire and rest. Let me remember the pleasant things from Paraíso,' Celina pleaded.

There would be other memories, not so pleasant, that she would remember too, whether she wished it or not, she thought as they walked hand in hand past the resinous Lignum vitae trees and the roses, some still in full bloom despite the lateness of the season. That first time, aboard Nicholas's ship, when she had discovered she was capable of love—deep, searing passion that threatened to rule her life unless she was strong enough to control it. Those times in the house when he had subjected her to his searching kisses and she had come close to losing that control. Yesterday beside the stream, when he had offered her wealth and position at his side, without telling her how short-lived it was to be, and she had flung unwarranted insults in his face in order to escape him. He had every right to despise her for the accusations—as she despised herself for wanting him so desperately, shamelessly.

A low moan off to their right brought them both to an abrupt standstill. It was the sound of someone in pain. They found Sulai lying partly hidden beneath some bushes. Her clothes were torn, her face and body bruised and bleeding. She was barely conscious. As they looked at each other in silent horror, both knew what had happened to her and who had perpetrated the despicable act.

'I'll take her upstairs. Xavier will go mad when he sees her,' David said, lifting her into his arms. 'I wish my services were required here under different circumstances. You must send someone after Nicholas and his father. I'm sure Xavier will go after Leclerc, and he will have murder in mind if he catches him.'

'I'll go. I'll take one of the horses. Don't argue, Davie
. . . I'm here and I know exactly where to find them.'

She roused one of the stable-lads and told him to
saddle a horse. Minutes later she was flying down the
'floral mile' towards the old house, praying, as she rode,
that Nicholas and his father had not decided to get drunk
together as Xavier had thought. The first spots of rain
fell on her as she passed the drying-sheds. It was fast
growing light, and men were beginning to stir, with
somewhat less enthusiasm than usual after an exuberant
night of wine-drinking and celebrating.

'Have you seen Jean Leclerc?' Celina cried, reining in
beside a man who stared at her sleepily, rubbed his eyes
and stared again at the young woman in a white brocade
evening gown, silver slippers on her feet, astride a
snorting flame-coated stallion.

'No, miss. Not since yesterday afternoon.'

'Keep an eye open for him. He's attacked one of the
women back at the house. Detain him and bring him to
Captain Benedict if he shows himself.'

The rain began to fall heavily, soaking her to the skin.
Wet tendrils of hair plastered her face and she had to
continually wipe them from her eyes. She could hear the
sound of the sea, although there was such a heavy mist
rising up from the ground, it was difficult to see the path
ahead. She was almost there!

A shape leapt out in front of her, catching the bridle of
her horse. At the same time, a rough hand fastened in
her skirts, dragging her sideways. She screamed as she
felt herself falling, and clutched wildly at the pommel of
the saddle, only to be wrenched savagely from the
horse's back. The ground came up to meet her with a
sickening thud which knocked the breath from her body.

There was a sharp pain at the back of her head and then blackness . . .

The rain on her face revived her. The noise she could hear in her head was no more than the sound of rain-drops on the leaves and trees about her, but it sounded like cannon-fire to her ears. She raised her head and cried out at the sudden pain and blurring of her vision. How long had she been lying here? There was no sign of her horse. He had taken it. She had no doubt her assailant had been Jean Leclerc. Now he had a horse and no one would catch him to bring him back to answer for the vicious beating of Sulai.

She had to get help. She stumbled to her feet, reeled unsteadily, and fell back into the mud which covered her bare arms and dress. On the third attempt she managed to sustain herself upright and staggered off along the path, guided by the continual noise of the sea ahead of her. Rain lashed her face, accompanied by a fierce wind which tore her hair free of the last remaining comb and blew it about her face in wild disorder. She lost count of how many times she slipped and fell, heaved herself upright again and went on. The path seemed endless. Surely she was not going in the wrong direction?

A horse whinneyed some way ahead and she came out of the thick trees to find the house in front of her. So great was her relief, that huge tears rolled unnoticed down over her already wet cheeks. She tried to call out, but could not raise a loud enough cry to attract attention over the lusty howl of the wind. Tripping over the torn hem of her gown, she dragged herself wearily up the steps to the veranda, fell against the door, her strength failing her . . . and her senses faded once more.

'Celina.' It was Nicholas's voice, far off in the distance. She opened her eyes, but could not distinguish his features. They swam and blurred before her tortured vision. 'Celina, for the love of God, girl, what has happened to you?'

'Give her some more brandy,' she heard another voice urge. That of his father.

'No.' How weak she sounded. 'Jean—attacked Sulai . . . Xavier has gone after him. He—he stopped me on my way here . . . took my horse . . .'

Nicholas swore as he laid her gently back on to the cushions, and the hand he drew away from behind her head was streaked with blood.

'Get her back to the house quickly,' John ordered. 'I'll get my men to scour the area. Leclerc won't get far.'

'I want him stopped,' Nicholas said, and his voice shook. 'I don't care how you do it, but I want him stopped and brought to me. He's going to pay for this night's work.'

Celina had drifted back into a state of semi-consciousness again. Nicholas had wrapped her in his cloak for warmth but, even so, several long shudders ran through her body. Cold or fear? He was shocked at the cold, murderous rage inside him. At this moment he knew he could have killed Jean Leclerc and not lost a night's sleep over it. Had he been in the room with them, he would not have been able to keep his hands from his throat.

'He could not get at Marianna, so he unleashed his spleen on any unfortunate woman he encountered. First Sulai, now Celina . . . He does not deserve to live.'

'He does not, Captain.' Dripping wet, Xavier had come unnoticed into the room. The black face bore signs of a fight. One eye was almost closed, his mouth cut and bleeding. His gaze rested on Celina. 'She is badly hurt?'

'A head wound. Where have you been, man?' Nicholas demanded, starting up, knowing the answer before Xavier gave a shrug of his broad shoulders. 'You found Leclerc?'

'I have come to give myself up to you, Captain. You will give me justice, speak for me if necessary, won't you?' It was not a plea for mercy, more a request from a friend, and Nicholas nodded. 'He is dead. I have killed him. He will disturb the peace of Paraíso no longer, Captain.'

Nicholas looked down into the ashen face of the unconscious girl before him, and his father saw a look of pain come into his eyes before he bent and gathered her into his arms, cradling her against his chest as tenderly as he might a new-born child. And it was then John Benedict realised why his son had sought to keep Celina MacNeill at his side.

CHAPTER
TEN

CELINA CRIED out in the terror of her nightmare. Those
last days in the heather before Cumberland's troops
captured them was with her again. David had been
forced to carry her when the last of her strength failed.
He had little to spare, yet still he urged her on when she
lagged, scooped her up in his arms and carried her when
her legs gave way beneath her, ignoring her protests to
leave her behind. The soldiers captured thirty women,
children and half-starved men too weak to put up resistance. She watched many of them cut down without
mercy, the women abused, children so cruelly treated,
many died on the journey to Inverness. She herself had
been spared only because David had told the officer in
charge who they were, and he had held back both
himself and his men in the hope of monetary reward
from some grateful relative who would come forward to
pay for their safe return. Neither told him in the beginning there was no family left to help them, and for two
whole months they were treated with some courtesy at
least.

The MacNeills of Craig Tor were not unknown to the
English. They had been instrumental in rousing many in
the surrounding glens who otherwise might not have
come forward to fight. Once all her jewellery had been
sold, leaving nothing with which to bribe their gaoler,

they were transferred back to a common gaol and treated like all the other wretches awaiting trial. Certain death awaited them, Celina was sure. She stayed beside her brother, despite all his entreaties to save herself. When they dragged him from the cell, bleeding and, she thought, dying, she gave up wanting to live. Perhaps that was why she had survived transportation. The face of the second officer swam in her nightmare, mocking as he moved towards her, intent on reducing her to a quivering, submissive wreck of a woman as he had done with many others on board. Then his face was covered in blood, and her screams echoed and re-echoed through her brain. She could feel the whip he had brought with him cutting her shoulders and then, when she had not uttered a sound, he had thrown it down and attacked her with his fists, kicked and pummelled her until she lay unconscious.

Someone moved her. She moaned in agony and terror and tried to push away the arms that cradled her.

'Leave me. Leave me,' she begged, writhing in her agony.

'Hush. Lie still, my little Scots cat. No one is here to harm you.'

Only one person had ever called her that. She opened her eyes, which felt so heavy she could scarcely raise the lids, and found his face above hers. It was his arms who held her, laid her with such gentleness back amid the pillows.

'Sleep. You are in no danger. Sleep now.'

No danger! Only from him. From herself, if she allowed him to know of her love. He would use her as others had sought to do. Her feelings would not matter.

'Davie . . .'

'I'm here, lass. Sleep. I'll stay beside you.'

She drifted back, unbeknownst to her, into a heavily drugged sleep, her brother's fingers laced tightly through hers. Ten minutes later David disengaged them and rose from the bedside. He looked at the still figure some feet away and wondered at the other side of this man he had glimpsed for a few minutes. There was no sign of that other person now. Nicholas's face was unreadable, wiped clean of the tenderness exposed earlier.

'She will not stir until mid-day tomorrow. Neither will Marianna. You will tell her the truth?'

'Yes. If she wishes to make a new life with you she has to accept what has happened.'

'You—you are not going to oppose us?' David was startled. He had expected opposition from the very beginning. 'I want to marry her, you realise that?'

'Give her time to get over what has happened, and then you can.' Nicholas dragged his eyes away from the still form in the large bed. He suddenly felt very tired, yet in need of company.

'Come and have a drink, MacNeill. We both need one.'

He followed Nicholas downstairs, disturbed by what he knew he must do. It could ruin his relationship with Marianna, it would harm the one he had with Nicholas, but he knew he had to make his feelings quite clear. Celina had suffered enough.

'You are going to let my sister go, then? Sell her to that old woman who wants her?'

'That is none of your concern.'

'You have said that before. You said Celina was to be your concern. You are easily distracted, Captain.'

'I'm in no mood to quarrel with you, MacNeill.' Nicholas glared at him, thrust a glass of brandy out to him, said tersely, 'Drink this and then let's both of us get some rest.'

'Not until I know what you intend for my sister,' David insisted stubbornly.

'I'm giving her the freedom she desires. She can leave here a free woman. She'll have money to go wherever she wishes.'

'So she was right. She was merely a diversion for you until you marry your mistress in Kingston?'

'Marry?' Nicholas's eyes gleamed with a strange light. He put his glass aside, untouched. 'She thinks that?'

'That's why she wants to leave. Not a very subtle approach, if I may say so. Dearest Celina, be my mistress until I marry and bring another woman to Paraíso! Don't you realise what this place has come to mean to her? Are you that blind, man?' David demanded, his face reddening with anger. 'In your way you have humiliated and abused my sister more than any man I've ever known. I don't think you've laid a hand on her, but that doesn't matter. There's something between you that I don't understand. My God, I wish I did. I'd like to end it. She doesn't deserve the unhappiness you have brought her for loving you . . .'

'Yes, child, dead,' Sulai repeated, as Celina stared at her open-mouthed. 'My man went after him and killed him. He did not intend it, at least I like to think he does not have that kind of temper. The captain's father took the body out to sea. Everyone will be told Jean Leclerc had an accident on board ship and was buried at sea. Who will question it? A whole ship's crew will vouch for the word of John Benedict.'

'Oh, Sulai, I am so glad that hateful man will not harm you any more, or Marianna,' Celina breathed. Two days had passed since she had been brought back to the house unconscious. Two days of living in a frightening dream-world she thought long forgotten. Such nightmares again . . . Sulai looked into the pale face and smiled. The bruises on her cheeks were fading, and the blouse she wore covered those on her arms and shoulders. Celina marvelled at her control after undergoing such an ordeal. She felt as weak as a new-born kitten and her head still ached abominably.

'Marianna?' She wanted to ask after Nicholas, but dared not. 'She knows?'

'Not yet.' Nicholas came into the room and motioned Sulai to leave. He came close to the bed and looked down at Celina, enquiring politely, 'Do you feel well enough to get up? For a few minutes only. I have to break the news of Jean's death to Marianna, and I'm not sure she is strong enough to withstand the shock. I would not ask you if I did not consider your presence necessary.'

'I am quite well,' Celina assured him, thrusting the throbbing of her head into the distance. Poor Marianna. The shock of what had happened might set back her progress for months. 'Please, hand me my robe, over that chair.'

He turned his back while she slipped on the blue silk robe and belted it around her waist. The blood drained from her face as she stood up and the room reeled around her. Turning, Nicholas gave a low oath and steadied her.

'No, I ask too much of you. Get back into bed.'

'Indeed I shall not, Captain Benedict. I would not have you tell my new owner that I shirk my responsibilities at the slightest opportunity.' Even in her weak state, she remembered what he was about to do to her.

His lips tightened at the jibe, but to her surprise there was not the answering retort she expected. David was in Marianna's room. She suspected he had been there since the night of the party, jealously guarding his newly-discovered love. How she envied him his freedom to choose his life, the woman who would be at his side. She knew her brother well. He would have Marianna despite all opposition, no matter which quarter it came from. And if she was strong enough to stay with him . . .

'Celina!' Tears ran unchecked down over Marianna's cheeks as she saw the other girl. She held out her arms and Celina ran to them, and for a long while they sat and hugged each other, oblivious of the presence of anyone else. 'Let me look at you! Have you recovered? Nicholas said you had a nasty knock on the head. What are you doing out of bed? You should be resting.'

'I am quite well now,' Celina assured her. She sensed that Marianna was greatly agitated, and the keen way in which her brother was watching her confirmed her suspicion.

Nicholas came round to the other side of the bed and perched himself on the edge, and instantly Marianna's eyes flew to his face questioningly.

'What is going on? What are you all keeping from me? I have been petted and fussed over for two whole days and no one has said a word about Jean. Where is he? Has he gone?' Her voice rose sharply, and Nicholas's hand sought hers above the counterpane.

'He has gone and he will not be back. Is that not the way you wanted it, little sister?' he asked gently.

'Yes . . . But he will be back, I know him. He will not let me be happy.'

'There is nothing he can do to prevent it. He is dead.'

Marianna gasped and fell back on to the pillows.

'You? Oh no, Nicholas, tell me it was not you?'

'No. Nor MacNeill. There was an accident. He stole a horse and it threw him. Xàvier discovered the body near our boundary fence.'

'No,' Marianna cried, her tone growing hysterical. 'It's not true. I know it. That's how Soledad died and you went after her that night, too.'

A momentary flicker of pain crossed Nicholas's face. Was he never to be allowed to forget that night? There had been murder in his heart when he pursued Soledad from the house, but he had not touched her. Her own wildness had resulted in her riding her horse too close to the cliff edge. Both rider and mount had plunged to their deaths on the beach below.

'Tell her the truth,' Celina urged quietly. 'Must they be forced to build a new life on half-truths and suspicions, as I have done?'

His eyes met hers and the challenge in them reduced her to silence. When have I ever forced you? they demanded. Many times, she could have told him. Not force of arms, or superior strength, but the force of his personality which had enmeshed her with invisible chains. When those she wore on her wrists had been removed the day he had bought her in Antigua, he had said she would never wear them again. Yet she was still chained! To him! To Paraíso! Even though she was preparing to give up both, she would remain linked to them wherever she went.

'Celina is right, as always.' He returned his attention to his sister. 'What I am going to tell you is not pleasant, Marianna, but I think you are strong enough to withstand the shock. You have proved that in these past few weeks, and I am so proud of you.'

'You—you are going to tell me Jean was unfaithful. I

know. I've always known.' She smiled at him briefly. She was safe! Free! The dread which had haunted her disappeared and her spirits lifted and soared in hope and anticipation. Now it was time for the truth. Her life with David MacNeill would have no shadows upon it. 'I did not have the courage to tell you. I was a coward.'

'Then it will come as no surprise to you to know he tried to force himself on Sulai before he left. She resisted and he beat her. It was Xavier who went after him, and, in the ensuing fight, Jean was killed. I believe Xavier when he says he did not mean to kill him. He was mad with rage, he admits that. In his position I would have reacted the same way.' Nicholas squeezed her fingers, his expression softening. 'There will be no unpleasantness for you. Jean's body was taken on board Father's ship and buried at sea. If anyone asks, we will say that Jean had an accident on his way to Kingston.'

'Father did that—for me?' Marianna asked in bewilderment. 'Oh, Nicholas, and I have been so hateful to him.'

'He was to blame for much of what you felt for him. He accepts that. But it is time now for you to get to know each other. He loves you very much and wants dearly to show it, but after all these years, he is afraid you will reject him.'

'When he held me downstairs I felt so brave. He made me take that first step! I was too much of a coward to do it alone, much as I wanted do. Afraid of myself, my husband . . .'

'My poor little Marianna,' Nicholas whispered, and touched her fingers to his cheek in an affectionate caress. How she longed to be in Marianna's place and have him touch her again, Celina thought sadly as she watched them. Gentleness was in him for her, for Joanna his future wife, but not for the servant-girl he desired without love. 'Be happy in whatever you do from this day onwards. Don't allow the past to dwell in your mind. Unless I am very much mistaken, you have the love of a fine man. Let MacNeill make you forget that Jean ever existed . . . with my blessing.'

'But he did,' Marianna insisted. 'And, because of him, I shut you out, allowed you to think it was you who drove me away from the inn in Kingston that day. I was not running from you, Nicholas, but from him. I did not tell him that you had threatened to cut off my allowance, that I would have no money of my own . . . not until after we were married. I thought he loved me and wanted nothing else. How naive of me, wasn't it? The change in him was . . .' She broke off with a shudder, and it was several minutes before she was able to continue. 'He drank heavily, swore at me. He said that I had nothing more to offer him and he would be leaving in the morning. I wanted to die! I knew you had been right. I had never meant anything to him. When you arrived, I panicked. I could not face you and tell you the truth, and so I fled. You know the rest. The horses bolted and the carriage overturned, throwing me out. When I recovered back here at Paraíso to find you had installed Jean as overseer so that he could be near me . . . I was terrified. He threatened me with such awful things if I confided in you. For weeks I lay here dreading every day that dawned.' She smiled at her brother again, this time through a mist of tears. 'I have grown up, Nicholas. I suddenly feel very old.'

'I wanted to make up for my harshness. I thought you loved him,' Nicholas said in a hollow tone. She had suffered a whole year in silence! 'Were you so afraid of me?'

'Of Jean. At last I accepted I was safe as long as I remained in bed. After a while it ceased to matter. And then you brought Celina to me and I saw someone who had survived greater hardships and sufferings than I. She brought me new hope—and courage—and then David gave me his love, and to walk again became the most important thing in my life. Even if I had to go against Jean. Please say you forgive me?' she entreated.

'We have both been foolish and proud. There is nothing to forgive. Will you receive Father when he comes home this evening? Make your peace with him? Let us be a family again.'

'Yes. Oh, yes. Downstairs. He shall see me walk again.'

'Only if I think you are strong enough,' David added sternly. 'I am first and foremost your doctor and you must still do as I say.'

'You are also the man I love with all my heart, and that is why I will obey you—tomorrow. Tonight I must greet my father standing on my own two feet. After that I promise to be the most obedient and docile patient you have ever had—and the most loving wife, if you still want me. Give me tonight, David. I owe it to him.'

As he took her hand and carried it to his lips and then bent to brush his mouth over one cheek, his expression full of tenderness, Nicholas turned to look at Celina and she lowered her eyes so that he would not see the pain mirrored there.

'Do you think your sister is well enough to sit a horse, MacNeill?' he asked, and her head flew up again, eyes widening.

'Why—yes, I think so. Is your head troubling you, Celina?' David asked, coming across to lay a cool hand against her wrist. 'Pulse normal. I should say it is all right.'

'Yes, it is,' Celina admitted. 'But I do not think I could ride.' Why was he seeking her company? To tell her he had made arrangements for her to leave? Of course, he did not want to upset Marianna.

'Good. Perhaps you would like to change and join me downstairs. I will have two horses saddled.'

'Where are you going?' Marianna asked curiously.

'I thought perhaps Celina would like a last look at Paraíso before she leaves tomorrow,' Nicholas returned with a shrug of broad shoulders, and she gasped aloud.

'You have not let her go? Oh, Nicholas, how could you? Does Father know? Has he agreed?'

'It is nothing to do with him; Celina belongs to me,' her brother returned. 'Why are you getting angry with me? It is Celina's own wish to go away. Is it not?'

Those eyes, like the clear blue of the sky, centred on her again. Where was the compassion, the gentleness, she had seen in him a few minutes ago? Go, to wait on a cantankerous old woman who would run her life, or stay and be his plaything.

'Yes. You see, Marianna. I am using no force to make her go. I would prefer her to stay. I have grown as used to her as Paraíso. She will be sadly missed.'

Liar, Celina wanted to scream, and Marianna began to implore her to change her mind. He even had his sister believing his pretended concern. David said nothing. She wondered at his quietness. He had not once mentioned her decision to leave since she had told him why she must go. Tears sprang to her eyes. Brushing aside the hands Marianna extended towards her, she turned blindly away from the bed.

'I—I do not think I feel well enough to ride.' She could

not go with Nicholas. Why could he not let her go in peace?

'I shall expect to see you downstairs in ten minutes,' he said coldly. 'If you are not, I shall come and fetch you. There is something you shall see before you quit my house.'

Mutely, Celina went to her room. After tomorrow he would give her no more high-handed orders. The knowledge brought her no pleasure.

'Where are we going?' she asked, after they had been riding for some while. What could he show her that she had not already seen?

'I have to stop by the drying-sheds, then you will see. My company is so distasteful to you, Celina?'

'No.' She looked straight ahead, aware of his gaze, but refusing to acknowledge it. It had rained during the night and drops of water glistened on leaves and flower-petals like glistening tears. She inhaled deeply, feeling the fresh air sink deep into her lungs. They were near the cliffs, for she could hear seagulls and smell the sea. How she would miss all this! 'I see no necessity for this.'

'I do and, until you leave Paraíso, I am still your master.'

And afterwards, she thought, a knife turning inside her. You will always be my master. No man will ever own my heart as you do. I want no other man to own my body.

'Marianna and I have agreed she should wait three months before announcing her engagement to your brother. Will you not stay for her, Celina? For him? They dearly want it.'

'You yourself said that the sooner I leave Paraíso, the better,' Celina reminded him with quivering lips. He moved his mount closer to hers and immediately she swerved away. He gave a short laugh and made no attempt to repeat the process.

'I spoke in haste. I was angry.'

'Because I would not become your mistress at the picnic? Would it not be a short-lived affair, sir? Are you not soon to be married?'

'I am.' His cool effrontery took her breath away. He considered her with narrowed gaze, and the light flickering in his eyes made her begin to tremble. He had looked at her the same way many times before when he had held her and kissed her. She was sure the only thing that had saved her on every occasion was the fact that he had not known how close she was to surrendering to his demands. 'I was hoping you would stay for the wedding. It will be the grandest affair Paraíso has ever seen. I intend to get married only once in my lifetime, and it will be a day I shall remember all my life. It's as it should be, don't you think?'

She could hardly speak. He wanted her to remain and watch him being married to another woman?

'Stay?' she echoed, her eyes growing frosty. 'In what capacity, sir?'

'I am sure we could find one which would be pleasing and satisfactory to us both. I have a great deal to offer you, Celina!'

'Not all that much, sir, as you would also be sharing with your wife. Would you not find that put a strain on even your resources?'

Her words kindled a spark of anger in his eyes and the lean mouth tightened visibly, but for a moment only. The smile she hated so much returned to mock her indignation and to tell her that she had not scored even a minor victory with her insult.

'Not in the least. My stamina would surprise you when

I am engaged in a pastime I enjoy,' came the infuriatingly tantalising answer, and she bit her lip in vexation. It was useless to try and talk to him further.

She remained silent as they rode the rest of the way to the sheds. He remained there with Xavier for nearly half an hour and returned without a word of apology for her long wait. The silence continued between them as they rode on to the cliff house. The 'Fox''s ship was in the bay, Celina noticed, and there seemed to be a great deal of activity going on. Longboats were being unloaded on the beach. Men were hauling timber and furniture up the cliff face and carrying it into the house. The garden had been freshly weeded, the roses trimmed and cut back. Several negroes were working there still. Another was putting a fresh coat of white paint on the veranda.

'My father has given me the house,' Nicholas said as they drew rein, and she looked at him, unable to hide the misery in her eyes. 'I intend to give it to my wife as a wedding present. Renovated, of course.'

His hands reached for her, grasped her round the waist before she could move back. With effortless ease he swung her to the ground, but he did not release her. His hands continued slowly up over her body, his fingers caressing the firm young breasts beneath the silk of her blouse, moving higher to where the curving neckline left arms and smooth shoulders bare to his touch.

'Please,' she entreated. If he touched her this way, she was lost. She must leave Paraíso! She would leave, but when she was so close to him she could not think, and her traitorous body began to enjoy his tantalising caresses. He was being deliberately provocative and she was helpless against the fires which swept through her. She closed her eyes, unable to bear the triumph in his eyes at the plea. He knew! She saw it written on his face and she felt faint with the knowledge that her one last barrier had gone. He would use her love to have his own way!

'Is it enough for you, Celina, or do you want more? There is nothing I would not give you to make you happy,' Nicholas murmured, and his lips lightly brushed the skin where moments before his fingers had lingered. Her eyes flew open, startled, unbelieving.

'What—what did you say? Is—is this some horrible joke?' she whispered and he gave an oath.

'You are mistress of my heart. Will you not also be mistress of Paraíso? Will you marry me and put this poor fool out of his misery?'

She gave a cry and fell against him, her senses swimming. Never in her wildest imagination could she have envisaged he had brought her here to ask her to marry him. What about Joanna? He was going to marry *her*? He had said so.

She opened her eyes a fraction, in time to see him carry her past the room where she had first met John Benedict. The walls were newly painted in pastel colours and there were bright velvet curtains at the windows. All the dust-covers had been removed and the floor polished with pine wax. Where was he taking her? Up the stairs and along the corridor where all the windows were thrown open to the sea. Her cheek rested against the smooth fabric of Nicholas's shirt. It smelt of tobacco and of man, and she did not want him to put her down, for then he would tell her she had been dreaming and he was to marry Joanna after all.

At the far end of the corridor he kicked open a door, carried her in and deposited her on the gigantic four-poster bed which dominated the room. She lay staring at him wide-eyed as he slammed the door shut and locked it behind him.

'What—what are you doing?' she stammered.

'I'm going to make sure you stay at Paraíso and marry me,' he returned grim-faced, as he advanced towards her. 'I shall do whatever I have to, Celina, to keep you with me.'

'You would not! Could not!' She screamed as he seized her, smothering her face and neck with kisses, holding her in an embrace from which she could not escape. It took a moment only to rouse her, and then she no longer wanted to flee. When he drew back from her, the cool blue eyes mocking and yet holding an expression of tenderness she had never seen for her, she discovered that her arms had been about his neck. Tentatively she touched the thick blond hair and instantly withdrew her fingers, colouring profusely. 'How did you know? I thought I hid it so well.'

'That you did. Too well. I was prepared to give you your freedom and let you go because I thought you were unhappy here. Had your brother not let slip your true feelings, I should have lost you. I must never lose you, Celina.' He buried his head against her, and his lips touched the rise of a breast above her blouse. She quivered at the intimate caress and he drew back, a smile touching his mouth. 'Tell me you will stay and be my wife and I shall not tease either of us any more. Not until our wedding-night,' he added wickedly.

'I love you. I think I have from that first day in Antigua. I hated you, too, for buying me. It seemed the final degradation at that time. I know different now.'

'So I am no longer your *bête noire*, eh?' Nicholas asked, stroking the curls from her flaming cheeks. The pliancy of her body crushed beneath his, the eagerness of her kisses, matching his, had aroused him far beyond anything he had ever known with any other woman, but he knew he must not take advantage of the moment. To wait, knowing she had known no other man before him, would bring the ultimate joy in his life. To possess her and bring satisfaction to them both would indeed make his wedding day one to remember for ever.

'You are my master,' Celina said tremulously, and he laid his lips against hers with a groan.

'No. Your slave. Haven't you realised that?'

'I—I thought you wanted me only for your mistress. I was afraid you would discover how I felt about you and use me, until you were married to her!'

'I don't love Joanna. I never have. I told her it was finished between us and that I was going to marry you. You were so distant, so contemptuous of me. I wanted you to fall into my arms with jealousy. Instead, I almost drove you away. Forgive me, my sweet. I wanted you so much, I would have done anything.'

'I shall spend the rest of my life extracting payment for all the misery you have caused me,' Celina said, eyes bright with tears. Tears of happiness which knew no bounds. 'You beast! You let me think, not an hour ago, that you wanted me to stay to be your mistress. How could you be so callous?'

'David said you loved me, but you showed little signs of it. I was desperate.' Nicholas kissed her for a long moment, moving alongside her on the huge bed, his arms twined round her as if he was afraid she would take to her heels and run. There was no chance of that, she thought, as she gave herself up to the delights of his lips, his hands.

'And you,' she said at great length, drawing back a little from him. 'How could you fall in love with me thinking me to be a—a wanton. A harlot?'

'I loved you from the first glimpse I had of you on the

quay at Antigua. You were the woman I would have as my wife. I can't explain it, I just knew; and so I bought you. I would have paid a hundred pounds to have you,' Nicholas returned in a fierce tone. 'Never underestimate me, Celina MacNeill. You are mine, but a man who has always known freedom will fight tooth and nail to keep it, as I did.'

'I have not sought to take it from you,' she said in surprise.

'Not knowingly, perhaps. Knowing it was inevitable, I fought against it all that much more strongly—and you. I know you are no wanton, that your colourful reputation is a lie that was brought down upon your head by unscrupulous men who needed to save their own hides and reputations.'

'How?'

He gave a soft chuckle as his fingers delved into the hollow between her breasts and she stiffened with a gasp.

'That's how, my little innocent. How little you know of life—of men. I had only to hold you and kiss you. A shameless wench would not have hesitated to use those times to her full advantage. Even when I discovered you were not what I had been told, I tried to convince myself otherwise. It made it easier to reject this hold you had over me. I no longer fight it, Celina, I am in your power and I revel in it. Say you will marry me before we have my father hammering on the door to rouse us?'

'He is here?'

'Waiting to be the first one to kiss my future bride.'

'Then we must not keep him waiting,' Celina answered, raising a hand to brush back her dishevelled hair. Her eyes sparkled with a sudden mischief. Reaching out, she locked her arms about Nicholas's head and drew his face to hers. 'I will marry you. I shall never love anyone else, never betray you, never leave you.'

'No more shall I,' Nicholas vowed, as his lips sought hers again. As her body curved into his, submissive, inviting, full of promise, he heard her softly say, 'I never want to be free. Be my master always.'

Mills & Boon

Your chance to step into the past Take 2 Books FREE

Discover a world long vanished. An age of chivalry and intrigue, powerful desires and exotic locations. Read about true love found by soldiers and statesmen, princesses and serving girls. All written as only Mills & Boon's top-selling authors know how. Become a regular reader of Mills & Boon Masquerade Historical Romances and enjoy 4 superb, new titles every two months, plus a whole range of special benefits: your very own personal membership card entitles you to a regular free newsletter packed with recipes, competitions, exclusive book offers plus other bargain offers and big cash savings.

AND an Introductory FREE GIFT for YOU. Turn over the page for details.

Fill in and send this coupon back today
and we will send you

2 Introductory
Historical Romances
FREE

At the same time we will reserve a subscription to
Mills & Boon Masquerade Historical Romances for
you. Every two months you will receive Four new,
superb titles delivered direct to your door. You
don't pay extra for delivery. Postage and packing is
always completely free. There is no obligation or
commitment – you only receive books for as long as
you want to.

**Just fill in and post the coupon today to MILLS & BOON
READER SERVICE, FREEPOST, P.O. BOX 236, CROYDON,
SURREY CR9 9EL.**

**Please Note:- READERS IN SOUTH AFRICA write to
Mills & Boon, Postbag X3010,
Randburg 2125, S. Africa.**

- -

FREE BOOKS CERTIFICATE

**To: Mills & Boon Reader Service, FREEPOST, P.O. Box 236,
Croydon, Surrey CR9 9EL.**

Please send me, free and without obligation, two Masquerade Historical Romances, and
reserve a Reader Service Subscription for me. If I decide to subscribe I shall receive,
following my free parcel of books, four new Masquerade Historical Romances every two
months for £5.00, post and packing free. If I decide not to subscribe, I shall write to you
within 10 days. The free books are mine to keep in any case. I understand that I may cancel
my subscription at any time simply by writing to you. I am over 18 years of age.

Please write in BLOCK CAPITALS.

Signature _____

Name _____

Address _____

_____ Post code _____

SEND NO MONEY — TAKE NO RISKS.

Please don't forget to include your Postcode.

Remember, postcodes speed delivery. Offer applies in UK only and is not valid
to present subscribers. Mills & Boon reserve the right to exercise discretion in
granting membership. If price changes are necessary you will be notified.

4M   Offer expires December 24th 1984.

EP9